I0604851
Flat Sole Studio
St. Paul, Minnesota

Flat Sole Studio
St. Paul, Minnesota
flatsolestudio.com

Library of Congress Cataloging-in-Publication Data
Library of Congress Control Number: 2024935613
ISBN: 978-1-0881-1608-1 (Ingram pbk)
ISBN: 979-8-324852-71-9 (Amazon pbk)

Credits
Blake Hoena, editorial direction
Flat Sole Studio, cover design and book layout

Image Credits
Shutterstock, cover

The
LAST STOP

Michael Loyd Gray

Spring, 1985

One

Art Millage had been police chief of Argus, Illinois, for fifteen mostly quiet years. But one day in May, when cool spring lingered, he abruptly left the police station. He drove to Lake Argus and stared into the water. As he wiped tears, he slipped and fell in the mud, soiling his uniform. He struggled to his feet, slipped again, and sat down hard and decided to stay there a spell. He shivered and breathed heavily.

He looked around but saw no one.

When he had caught his breath, he sobbed again and tucked his knees tightly up under his chin and rocked, his palms caked with mud, and realized he had no idea what his grief might be, or why he was crying.

Slowly, he uncoiled.

Awkwardly, he got up.

Art washed his hands in the cold lake water. He brushed his uniform with a rag from his police car. A chattering loon sailed around the near point, bobbing its head foolishly. There were no boats on the lake. No cars trundled across the long white causeway. The water gurgled obscenely as it lapped jagged rocks along the shore by his feet.

He felt a chill and shook again.

Art drove home, still shaky. The house was a brick ranch shaded by tall sycamores. It nested in a narrow bay of Lake Argus.

It was afternoon and Carolyn, his wife, was still at Argus High. She taught English, and he knew that on this day she had a faculty meeting that would run long.

He showered and lingered under the warm water, the steam enveloping him in a protective, foggy cocoon. It restored him. He felt better and studied his face in the bathroom mirror: he saw a man still handsome with a full head of brown hair parted on the left side. He looked younger than fifty-three, but the remnants of the day's anguish persisted and glowed in the corners of his eyes and mouth.

He changed out of his dirty uniform and was putting on a clean one when he decided instead for jeans, a crisp blue oxford shirt and new tennis shoes. He grabbed the muddy uniform and went down to the laundry room in the basement and stuffed it in a hamper, hoping Carolyn wouldn't likely see it for a while. He had time to come up with a plausible explanation.

Then he drove west, toward the dipping sun, among the smaller towns of his county. He stopped once to eat chicken fried steak and mashed potatoes at a diner in a town he had never visited before. When he got home, much later that night, Carolyn was asleep. Art slipped off his clothes and slipped into bed quietly without waking her.

He fell asleep almost immediately.

Two

The next morning, Art looked up from his desk and saw Red Foley, one of his deputies, striding down the hall toward him. Red was pale-skinned, wiry, and sported a fiery red crew cut. His first name was Arthur., but Art had decided that two Arts in the department were three too many. So, Red became Red and rather liked it, he often said, though Art often thought Red resembled a strutting human rooster. It was early, and Art was still on his first coffee. He took another sip and beat Red to the punch as he walked in the door.

"Red, what's got your shorts in a bunch so damn early?"

Red stopped abruptly in the doorway and placed his hands on his hips. Art thought that he looked a little hurt.

"Now, Chief, who says my shorts are in a bunch? Was it Bill?"

Art was amused at how quickly Red could get his blood up.

"I haven't seen Bill yet this morning, Red."

"Okay, then it was Scotty Simms—had to be."

"Scotty has the day off," Art said. "What can I do for you so early?"

Red shifted weight from one leg to the other for a moment, and then spat it out:

"It's Old Lady Thomas. That's what has me going this damn morning."

"I see," Art said quietly.

"She called again, Chief—she's seeing things again, out on that damn farm of hers."

Art was already visualizing Maggie Thomas and her farm, the tall, imposing farmhouse on a rise.

"She called this morning?"

"Just now, Chief."

Art smirked.

"What'd she say she's seeing out there—on that damn farm?"

"What she always sees—Martians, for all I know. Or care."

Art smiled slightly. He knew very well that Red was a bit of a zealot, barely contained, prone to impulse. Red wanted action, to fight crime, but crime was in short supply in sleepy Argus, which was why Art was there at all and had been for fifteen years, following ten as a Chicago cop. There was just the one incident, his first year in Argus, and it had been bad enough. Very bad. He'd had to shoot someone who had shot at him. But there was no time to go down memory lane on that one. No need, either. He hoped.

"What'd you tell Old Lady—Mrs. Thomas?" Art said, leaning forward and dropping elbows on his desk. He really had to get Red off calling her that.

"Not much," Red said. "I said I'd let you know about it."

Art stared at Red and Red looked away after a couple of seconds.

"Red?"

"Okay, Chief—I told her you'd go out there and have a look."

Art nodded, slumped back again into his chair.

"But that's why I have deputies, Red. That's why I have you, my friend."

Red glanced at the floor.

"Sorry, Chief.

Art shrugged.

"That's okay, Arthur." Art was mildly surprised he had called him that.

Red looked up sharply.

"But she likes you, Chief. At least I think she does. I don't think she really likes anybody, but she does seem to listen to you. When we go out there, she calls us underlings. I hate that word."

Art smiled.

"So would I."

And then he recalled the previous day's events, the crying, not knowing why he had cried, and he frowned heavily. His stomach churned and his palms sweated.

"You okay, Chief?" Red frowned, too. "Chief?"

Art snapped out of it.

"What?" Art said.

"You looked distracted, Chief."

Art pushed away from the desk and stood up slowly.

"Sorry. I guess I've got a few things on my mind."

"You looked a little pale," Red said. "You feeling okay?"

Art studied Red's face and felt he saw genuine concern.

"I'm just fine," Art said. "Don't worry about it." He didn't know what to do with his hands and finally he shoved them into his pants pockets. "What did you really tell Maggie Thomas?"

Red hung his head and shrugged.

"I told her you were already on the way. Sorry about that. But she really busts our balls when we go out there."

Art nodded and pondered for a moment that his deputies were afraid of an 80-year-old woman with arthritic hips who lived alone on a farm, save for two sons who worked the place but lived over in Kelton.

Red looked like a boy hoping his father would excuse him from having to mow the lawn on a sizzling day.

Art squeezed Red's shoulder lightly.

"Well, then I guess I'd better head out there and see what Maggie wants."

Three

Flimsy rain followed Art out to the Thomas farm, but it relented as he pulled up the lane to the farmhouse. It was a very old two-story, Italianate, as Art understood it, and built in 1850. The original owner had died at Shiloh in the Civil War with an Illinois regiment. Heroically, so the story went. The house was a majestic, towering old thing, with a wide porch and tall supporting columns. To Art, it conveyed the notion of a battered but defiant old frigate tied up to a dock.

He got out of the car and walked toward the house. The rain had dampened the lane. Maggie Thomas was already coming out the front door. She used a cane, but got around with it quite nimbly, Art noticed. Maybe it was the cane that his deputies feared. *Thank God for them this isn't Chicago.* He shook his head at the thought. Absently, he rubbed a finger on his cheek, the one where a bullet fired on Chicago's South Side had barely kissed and stung him in a dark alley. That had been the sting that propelled him to Argus.

"Chief," she said. She waved the cane, but Art knew her well enough to recognize it as a welcoming gesture. It always put his deputies on the defensive, though, and that's where misunderstandings got started.

"Hi, Maggie. You're moving on your pins today like a dancer."

She paused and smiled, brandishing the cane above her head like it was a battle axe.

"I do okay for an old lady with bad hips and a grumpy temper."

"You sure keep my deputies on their toes. I'll give you that."

She laughed.

"Oh, hell—it does them good, Chief. Especially that Red. He needs someone to bring him down a little from time to time. He's haughty."

Art reached the steps and gripped one of the columns.

"He's young—still trying to know his butt from a hole in the ground."

Art knew that Maggie relished earthy talk, and she wasn't opposed to swearing like a drunken sailor sometimes. Art had been a drunken sailor a few times during the last year of the Korean War.

Maggie waved the cane.

"By damn, Chief, I told that Red one day I'd poke that wide butt of his if he didn't show some respect."

Art winced and then smiled. He had to admit the image was funny. And he was fairly sure Maggie would do it, too. His deputies had reason to be afraid, after all. But more than anything, Art knew that Maggie Thomas just needed someone to talk to from time to time. Her sons worked the farm reliably but had families and full lives that consumed them. Maggie's husband had been dead for ten years.

Art sat on one of the steps, and Maggie waddled down them and sat next to him, the cane across her lap. He slowly and gingerly grasped the cane and placed it between them on the steps.

"Maybe we give the old hickory a rest, too," Art said gently.

"You know best, Art. I reckon that's a good idea. And I need to have a load off, too. Been puttering around the house all morning."

She sagged into the step. Neither spoke for almost a minute. Art studied the cornfield across the county road. The Thomas boys would be planting soon. They would want some more rain as soon as possible. But he also had fleeting thoughts of the day before when he felt so out of sorts and cried and then had to drive the county for hours as though there was someplace he had to be, or wanted to be, but he didn't know where it was. It made his stomach queasy again.

Art spoke first, soothingly.

"So, Maggie. What's it about? What can I do for you this morning?"

She cleared her throat.

"Red probably told you I was seeing Martians again."

Art chuckled.

"That he did. Sorry. But I never believe him, of course. Martians wouldn't choose Argus—too much corn and humidity."

"They'd pick California, Art—out there with all the nuts and such."

"That's right. No worries about Martians around here."

Maggie squeezed Art's elbow.

"I never see Martians, Art. Truly I don't. I don't know where that boy got that. But sometimes, I do see my little sister."

Art only knew she had a dead sister and not much more than that. He mulled it a moment.

"What was her name?" he finally said.

"Lucinda. Lucy. Sometimes, Lucy Jean."

Art didn't like where it was going but knew it was going there anyway.

"How old was she—Lucy Jean? When she passed, I mean."

"Only ten. Just a ten-year-old girl. I was fifteen."

He did the math quickly in his head.

"Been a while," he said. "A long time ago. Well before my time, Maggie."

"It was 1920," she said. "The first war—the one they said was the last one—was still a fresh memory. My daddy got nicked up some over in France with the Marines at Belleau Wood." She looked out over the fields. "Some days, though, it seems like yesterday. Or just this morning."

"I can imagine," he said, though he really couldn't. "I mean, I'm sorry."

After a spell she said, "You served in a war, didn't you, Art?"

He nodded.

"Korea. I was in the Navy. I was as haughty back then as maybe Red is."

She cackled and slapped his knee.

"I bet you weren't. You always seem sensible."

He wondered if that was true.

"Oh, I was probably just like Red, I'm sure. I was just a skinny kid from Chicago who thought nothing could scare him. I thought I knew it all."

"Was it bad, Art–the war?"

"No. Not for me, anyway. I was on a supply ship. Pretty boring, monotonous. We heard the war but didn't see much of it. But I did learn to be scared a few times. Good lessons."

More silence.

Art said, "When you see your sister, what's that like?"

Maggie looked at him. He wondered what she saw in his face.

"It's pleasant, Art. Very pleasant. She has a rosy color in her cheeks and her blonde hair twirls some from a breeze. She's always smiling. That's the way she was."

Art didn't want to ask the next question.

"How did it happen?"

She smoothed the folds of her blue sun dress and clasped his hand. With her other hand, she pointed at the road where it joined the lane.

"There," she said. "Right there, at the bottom of the lane. She was chasing one of the dogs and didn't pay attention to her surroundings, I guess. An oil truck had come by, and she slipped and fell against it. She hit her head on hard metal. I ran over and she called my name twice—'Maggie Maggie.' And then she was dead, right there beside the road. Blood spreading out from her head, but her face was composed, almost angelic. I was fifteen and had lost my only sister and best friend in the whole world. Now she *is* an angel."

"And she comes to visit," Art said quietly.

"Yes, Art. Yes, she does, bless her young heart."

She gripped Art's hand hard and leaned against his shoulder and sobbed. He reached across her and pulled her closer with his free hand. He wanted to cry, too. It took all his willpower not to. He was surprised he didn't, felt a tear nonetheless streak down a cheek. He almost felt like just falling apart but managed to somehow hold it together. That was his job, after all—wasn't it?

He patted her shoulder and reminded himself to tell Red and the others to show Maggie more respect, even if she ever claimed to see Martians.

Four

Dr. Finch told Art he was fine.

"Fit as a fiddle, Chief. You seem to lean closer to forty than sixty." He patted his own ample belly. "I'm sixty-five and leaning toward retirement soon—and a much-needed diet."

"No surprises, Thad?"

"You're as strong as a horse."

"What happened to fit as a fiddle?"

"You're both. A horse that could play Brahms."

"Well, I guess I can't bitch about that. Might prefer Beethoven, though."

Dr. Finch finished writing on the chart.

"No, you sure can't bitch about it, Art. You look good—great blood pressure, good cholesterol." He touched Art's cheek. "Though, there is this pissant scar here. Barely noticeable. Childhood spitballs—something like that?"

Art impulsively ran his own finger along it and managed a weak smile.

"That's a forty-five caliber spitball. Almost seventeen years old. From back in Chicago."

Dr. Finch raised his eyebrows and then leaned close for a better look.

"Really? You have to look close to see it, though I could tell it didn't date to childhood. So, this was something before that business years ago, when you first got here? Goodness, Art. I didn't know there were two shooting incidents. I just know the one."

Art stiffened and glanced at the Johns Hopkins diploma on the wall.

"Brant Russell, you mean, Thad?"

Hearing himself say the name aloud was a shock. Art had not said that name in years.

"I remember it very well now," Dr. Finch said. "The paper kicked it around for a week or two."

"That's right, Thad—I've killed two people in the line of duty. I'm well aware of that. I had a lead role in those little dramas."

"But you apparently don't talk about them," Dr. Finch said. "Is that right?"

"That's right. I don't."

Art felt a flash of anger but managed to head it off. He instinctively tried hard not to let the past suddenly come back in a rush. Glimmers tried to break through anyway, and he saw enough of them to wish it all hadn't come up. He managed to tamp it back down into that dark place inside where the bad things were kept on ice.

Dr. Finch sat on a stool. Art buttoned his shirt.

"Well, Art, from the look of it, it was an incredibly close call. You're lucky. More than lucky, maybe. Half an inch closer and you would have had a damn serious wound. An inch closer and maybe you're one of the headless horsemen—sorry for that metaphor."

"The bullet gave me a little kiss. That's all. A little smack on the cheek. And it's a dandy metaphor. I know what they are."

Dr. Finch nodded.

"I didn't say you didn't, Chief. So, you really don't talk about it, that little kiss?"

"Should I?"

"Depends, Art. You came to see me saying you started crying for no reason. It's nothing physical, and you don't really seem clinically depressed to me, though I know a guy in

Bloomington you can go see about that. A family friend and highly recommended."

"A head doctor."

"Yes, a psychiatrist."

Art finished buttoning his shirt, eased off the table, and tucked his shirttail into his pants.

"No, I guess I don't really ever talk about it. Carolyn has never even asked about it. I can't say for sure she's ever noticed it. Or maybe she did and chalked it up to the battle scars we all accumulate. I've got a crooked toe I broke in the Navy."

"But did you get *shot* in the toe, Art?"

Art grinned.

"I stubbed it one night drunk in Seoul. My war wound."

Dr. Finch frowned.

"Sit back down a minute, Art. Would you do that?"

Art stared at him a moment, then nodded. "Okay. Sure." He scooted back on the table.

"Shoot, Doc."

"That's funny, Art."

"We have to laugh, otherwise we'd cry. Isn't that the saying? Or maybe just some dumb country song."

"And you've done the crying, Art. Now you're here. Physically, you could probably run a marathon as long as your ankles and that toe aren't balky for any reason. Tell me about Chicago. Tell me about that little kiss on your cheek."

Art leaned back and supported himself with his palms behind his back. In an instant, his mind relaxed just enough for him to see, for the millionth time, the muzzle flash in that dark alley. He felt the bee sting again on his cheek. He heard his own revolver exploding twice, aimed generally in the direction of the muzzle flash, as he lost his balance and toppled into bushes. He heard someone—a woman—yell something from an open second-story window in a building beside the mouth of the alley. He never could quite recall what her words were—just a scorching yell.

"And then it was quiet, Thad. I was staring up at the sky, on my back, and could see millions of stars. Billions, I suppose. What an amazingly clear night it was. Then I felt my cheek. It was wet, but after a moment I could tell it wasn't bad. Just like a bee sting. A sudden shock. I was breathing hard—and damn scared."

"And the man who shot you?"

Art looked past Dr. Finch, at an anatomy chart on a wall.

"It was a woman. One of my two rounds caught her—smack thud in the head. The frontal lobe, to be exact—since we're being exact here." Art found it on the anatomy chart. "A one in a million shot, really. Pure dumb luck."

"Dear Jesus," Dr. Finch said.

"Yeah, I talked to *him* about it, too, for quite some time after that, in churches around the South Side."

"Still?"

"No."

"Why not?"

"He didn't make it go away, so I finally stopped asking."

"Did you think he would?"

"There's always hope. Isn't that what faith is about?"

"Well, I suspect faith is about faith." Dr. Finch placed the chart on a counter. "Art, what faith are you?"

Here we go, Art thought.

"Doctor Finch, I'm not a Catholic, nor a Baptist, nor a Protestant, nor a Mormon."

"And yet I have seen you at Mass."

Art shrugged.

"Town politics. Being Chief means showing up at churches from time to time, like any other place where the good townsfolk expect to take the measure of the man who watches things while they sleep in their warm beds."

"I see. Art, are you finding it hard to live up to being measured—to being Chief?"

Art pondered it. Dr. Finch had crossed his arms across his chest and really did expect an answer. Art could see that. And the question was pointed. Hell, it was as sharp as a dagger. It might as well have been pressed to his throat. Smack against the jugular. It really was shaping up to be quite an anatomy lesson.

"I don't know." And Art felt it was true enough. "Sorry about calling Mass just politics, Thad. I didn't mean anything toward you on being Catholic. Not at all. I'm an equal opportunity rejecter of faith—organized faith, that is."

"Uh-huh," Dr. Finch said, and Art recognized it as a professional, uh-huh—very clinical, distant, probing.

Art thought of just leaving at the point—becoming the Chief again and using that officious presence to end to the conversation. It generally worked quite well. Keep a certain distance between the badge and the people it shielded. That was indeed a part of the job. But Art, too, had finally sensed that the distance might indeed be breaking down. Decaying. Maybe he was, too. Part of breaking down, he suspected, was being among the last to really understand it was happening.

"Thad, how hard can it be to be Chief, after all? I mean, we don't really have crime in Argus. None to speak of lately, anyway. A fight sometimes at Bunnie's Tavern when somebody drinks too much happyjack or plays grab ass with the wrong woman. Or maybe some high school kids pull some petty bullshit. Crime opportunities are kind of limited around here."

"Is that why you came here, Art—from Chicago? To still be a cop, but not have to *be* a cop, so to speak?"

Art bristled.

"I take care of the town. No one can say I don't. That little thing you alluded to from years ago? I took care of the town that day, too."

Dr. Finch reached over and patted Art's knee.

"Sorry, Art. Not what I meant at all. That came out wrong."

Art slipped off the table.

"I should go. Chief business and all that."

The doctor tugged Art's shirt sleeve.

"Art, you've killed two people as a cop. And we haven't talked at all about the second one."

Art gently pulled his sleeve free of the doctor's hand.

"And we won't be talking about that second one, doctor. Not today, anyway."

Art heard himself loud and clear.

He was the Chief again.

Five

Carolyn frowned at Art.

"Art, how did your uniform get so dirty the other day? It was soiled head to toe. Have you been mud wrestling?"

"I slipped in the mud. Down by Stevenson Point. No mud wrestling, as much fun as it sounds. Maybe we could try that some time."

She smiled thinly.

"You didn't mention it, though."

He shrugged his shoulders.

"Sorry. Maybe I should have. But there's nothing to mention, really. I slipped. End of story."

"What were you doing down at Stevenson Point?"

Art was prepared for that.

"I thought I saw something in the water. You know how the road and that little bridge there give you a good look at the shore? But it was nothing."

Carolyn sat on the loveseat opposite Art. He had one of her books, a poetry anthology, and he'd been reading Frost—"Stopping By Woods on a Snowy Evening." It had been many years since he had last read it. She wore a faded denim shirt and snug jeans that looked good on her, he thought. Her blonde hair lingered along the collar. It was a Saturday, and she had been grading essays in her study. She had a study, and Art had a little office, too, in the back of the house. They respected each other's space and ran the rest of the house jointly.

She had a puzzled look on her face.

"Art, what did you think you saw in the water?"

He forced a grin, tried to appear nonchalant, felt it seemed forced.

"Well, you never know," he said, clasping his hands in his lap as though attempting to pray. "It could be all kinds of things—an animal, for instance."

"Like a beaver?"

His face brightened.

"Could be—yes. Or maybe just a big dog."

She frowned. Art knew there was just so much smoke he could blow her way. She was a smart woman, intuitive.

"*Was* it a dog, Art?"

He felt the line of inquiry had gotten sharp.

"Like I said, it was actually nothing. Maybe driftwood. Who knows?"

He threw his hands up for emphasis.

"Were you looking for a body, Art? Did you think you saw a body?"

Art unclasped his hands and rose up a little on the sofa. The book slipped from his lap to the floor, and he leaned over awkwardly and picked it up.

"Sure—that crossed my mind," he said. "Stuff in the water can make you think of all sorts of things."

"Like what?"

"Well, before I was Chief, a guy killed himself by jumping in the lake. More than twenty years ago. A farmer going by on a tractor saw the body floating along shore."

She nodded, lifted her hair with both hands and let it fall again on her shirt collar.

"I recall that."

She sighed.

Art knew she was analyzing what he had said. That was her nature. She dealt with snot-nosed high school kids and their bogus arguments in poorly written essays, and she was good at sifting the chaff to find some wheat.

"You know," she said, "we often see things we want to see—things we're looking for."

He attempted diversion.

"Like ghosts, you mean? I think people who believe in ghosts end up finally seeing *something* because they want to see it. But it's all in the mind, I'd guess."

"Art, don't you believe in ghosts?"

"I've never seen one, so I guess I don't. I guess I never *wanted* to see one. But Maggie Thomas, that's a different story. She sees her long-dead little sister sometimes."

"I've heard she's sort of crazy," Carolyn said. "Too bad."

Art shook his head vigorously.

"She's lonely. Big difference."

Carolyn nodded and looked away for a moment, toward the kitchen.

Art doubted he was out of the woods yet. He didn't know what to do with the book and finally placed it on the sofa beside himself.

"I was reading Frost," he said quietly.

"Which one?"

Her face brightened.

"The one about stopping in dark woods—you know, a guy, his horse. Lots of snow."

He often pretended to not know the names of poems, but he knew them all right. He had gotten on to Frost in high school and remembered his poems, even in Korea, when there, too, it was dark and lonely.

She smiled slightly.

"Students like to think that one is about death—suicide."

Art had to admit he was never quite sure *what* it was about, though he loved the parts about miles to go before sleeping.

"It's a dark poem, for sure—and dark *in* the poem, too," he said. "I guess I can see how that comes up—death."

"Suicide," she said.

He hesitated, tried to evaluate the look on her face. It alternated between subtle amusement and something else not so easy to define. Not anger. He knew what that looked like. Concern, maybe.

"So, it's not really about death. Is that what you're saying, Carolyn?"

He really was curious.

She leaned forward, elbows on knees.

"Well, there is a subconscious desire—temptation, attraction—for death suggested in it, perhaps," she said. "But the speaker resists it."

That suddenly made sense to Art, and it pleased him. It was like solving an ages old riddle that had bedeviled him.

"Hey—I can see that," he said. "Like I said, I last read it years ago. But, yeah, all that makes some sense to me now."

She laughed.

"Art, why do you do that?"

But her tone was friendly.

"Do what?"

"You know, pretend to be, um, less intelligent than you are."

Using the same friendly tone, Art said, "Carolyn, are you calling me dumb?"

She looked slightly stricken and frowned and leaned across the coffee table and touched his hand.

"No, no, baby—not at all. But you were reading poetry when I first met you. I know you like it. I know you understand it, too. Do you think it's something you have to keep hidden from people to be the Chief?"

He leaned back in the sofa.

"I didn't go to college, Carolyn."

"What's that have to do with being smart?" she said.

He fidgeted, couldn't get settled on the sofa.

"I lied about my age and joined the Navy when I was just sixteen. I could pass for eighteen then."

"I know that, baby. I've seen the pictures. So what?"

"Well, damn, Carolyn—I went from high school to the Navy to Korea to Chicago cop, all when I was still a kid. I missed the education part. I missed—normalcy?"

"Normalcy might be overrated, Art. I'm pretty sure it is. You saw some of the world. You got educated that way."

"The old college of hard knocks, right? Yeah, maybe. Maybe. I don't know. But you, you have a master's in English from Illinois."

"So?"

He got up and paced around to the rear of the sofa and placed his hands on the back of it.

"I guess I'm saying if I was more formally educated—like you—people wouldn't think twice about poetry and stuff like that. I guess they do have certain expectations—perceptions—about what a Chief is. Who he is, what he does, how he thinks."

She got up and went to him and slipped her hands around his waist from behind. She nestled her face in the crook of his neck.

"Art, are you feeling trapped inside the Chief?"

Art gripped her hands at his waist and closed his eyes to fight tears. Was he? He feared the answer, kept it dammed up behind him as best he could.

"Babe, I just don't know. Maybe I am. Maybe I just can't admit it. But I'm getting this funny feeling I might start seeing ghosts, too."

They tightened the grips on each other's hands and stood there for some time, slowly rocking back and forth as if dancing.

Six

Within a week, Art had been right: he *was* seeing ghosts. Well, not actual ghosts—more precisely, memories of people from his past he could no longer stop visiting him. The first one was the woman he'd killed in that Chicago alley. Okay, she had a name, he forced himself to concede—Margo Townsend. She had been thirty-five and a heroin addict when he shot her after she robbed a White Hen Pantry with a forty-five tucked in her pants. He wondered, and half-seriously, too, whether he should go see Maggie Thomas and ask how the routine went when a ghost showed up. Pointers. Tips. What was the routine with ghosts? The etiquette?

Stop calling them that, he reminded himself. They weren't ghosts.

Victims.

And then he went out to Maggie's again anyway. She didn't answer the door, and Art found her working in her garden. She pushed the front of her Cubs baseball cap up higher on her head. She looked surprised to see him.

"Well, Chief. Howdy again. But I didn't call you gents. Or did I? Sometimes I can be forgetful."

"I was just in the neighborhood." Art walked over to the garden. "What are you planting?"

"Tomatoes, cucumbers, some of that Swiss chard I heard about. Thought I'd give it a try."

"Cucumbers in vinegar," Art said. "I always liked that."

"Then I'll set aside some for you when the time comes," she said. "And you tell that Red you were just out here in the neighborhood today."

Art grinned.

"Deal."

"But you weren't just in the neighborhood, Chief."

"No. Not at all."

"Some desperate desperado out this way you're looking for?"

Art thought, *I have known only the two desperate desperados in twenty years as a cop. Maybe that's a pretty good record. Something to build on.*

"Nothing so exotic, Maggie."

He looked out over the fields that would soon enough have sprouting cornstalks. It was a flat Central Illinois landscape that afforded a lot of sky and horizon. So different than Chicago. But less confining, too.

Maggie said, "My boys start planting any day now. I suspect they're a bit late, but not too late. They get busy with their families. I know that."

"Now's the time," Art said, though he really had little idea how to raise corn and soybeans. He only knew when farmers planted and that they wished for enough rain. The rich Illinois soil did the rest. He had grown up in Rogers Park, on Chicago's North Side. Not much corn farming up there. He didn't really know what soybeans were until he moved to Argus.

The day was warming up. Maggie wiped her forehead with the back of a hand.

"Chief, how about a cold beer? I've been working my way toward one."

Art almost said he was surprised to hear she drank beer, but suppressed it, didn't want to seem rude. Even though she was 80, she sure seemed in good health and a beer was her business. He'd had an uncle who lived to 95, and he had taken a drink or two of whiskey just about every day. He glanced at his watch: it was past noon—a silly custom—and he had had a good lunch of corned beef and cabbage at the VFW before coming out.

"Sure. I'd join you for a beer."

"Just one," she said. "I limit myself to one after working at something—a reward. Dr. Finch says one a day might actually be good for me. And you're on duty."

"I know. But I *am* the Chief. The prerogative of power, I suppose."

Maggie squeezed Art's elbow.

"Just between the two of us, Art, I think old Doc Finch sometimes is full of shit."

Art laughed loudly, and they walked to the front porch and Art sat in the swing while Maggie retrieved two Pabst Blue Ribbons. They were very cold and slippery from the condensation. Art took a healthy swig. Maggie sipped hers and sat in a large wicker chair.

"So, Chief—what can I do you for?"

He took another swig of beer.

"Do I seem like I need help?"

She nodded.

"I think there's something on your mind, Chief. You don't seem the type to just be in a neighborhood by accident."

"Art. Just call me Art, if that's okay. Don't you call Red— Red?"

She snickered, sipped more beer.

"I call him Junior Deputy Arthur Foley, just to needle him some."

Art smiled broadly.

"He rather likes being Red instead of an Arthur. I suspect he thinks Red has—panache."

"Do you think he knows what panache is, Art?"

"I seriously doubt it. I looked it up myself the first time I ever heard it."

"It's a good word, panache. It has a certain texture to it. Art, did you know I was once a schoolteacher?"

He'd had no idea but didn't find it hard to believe. He could imagine a much younger Maggie keeping errant schoolboys on their toes, like she did with his deputies. Perhaps using a yardstick instead of a cane.

"I didn't know. What did you teach?"

"Social studies. And a little English, too."

"In Argus?"

"Argus High. But that was thirty years ago. I retired at fifty."

"My wife, Carolyn, teaches English at Argus High."

"But does she make you cucumbers in vinegar?"

He finished the beer.

"I'll see if she will when you make good on your promise."

"Deal."

Maggie reached over with her can and they clinked them together.

The beer loosened Art's tongue just enough.

"Maggie, do you still see your sister? Forgive me if that's too personal—too blunt."

She shook her head.

"That's okay. We're on first names here and swilling beer together. It's okay to ask."

She glanced down at the lane, where it met the county road. She finished her beer and sat the can on the porch.

"Do you think it's crazy—seeing Lucy Jean?"

He remembered that Carolyn had said it was. But Carolyn didn't know Maggie.

"I don't, no."

He believed that.

"I bet that Red does."

"Red's got a lot coming to him yet. He's only twenty-five."

She cackled softly.

"I can't even remember twenty-five."

"It does seem a little far off to me, too."

"You were back from the war by then?"

"Oh, sure. I was back from Korea and knocking around Chicago, doing different jobs, not sure where I was going. Just getting by, but not needing so much, either. I was still a kid. This was before I got on the Chicago force."

Art noticed she seemed to be assessing him, studying his face.

"Who are *you* seeing, Art?"

He was slow to pick up on it.

"Excuse me?"

"From the past. Whose ghost has come calling on you? I figure that's why you're out here."

He hadn't realized just how nervous he would feel when it was finally time to own up to the past. He thought of asking for another beer, but that would be a mistake. It would make him seem a little desperate—weak, perhaps. There was an example to set for his deputies. For the whole town, really. It was a hard standard to live up to, and he had been doing it for many years. For the first time, he was openly admitting to himself he was unsure how much longer he could do it. It scared him. If he couldn't be Chief, who could he be?

"I don't see ghosts, Maggie. Neither do you."

She chewed her lower lip.

"I know that. We call them that, but really they're just memories. Red thinks I must be crazy and seeing apparitions and such. Spooks rattling the chandeliers and the silver. But it's just memories. Vivid memories. We need them to survive. Who are you remembering, Art?"

He climbed out of the swing and leaned against one of the porch columns. Standing was better, he decided. The swing moved too much, and he needed to do something with his hands. He finally settled against the railing and used his hands to support himself.

"No one special," he lied, looking down at the porch floor.

She reached over and patted his knee.

"Do you want another beer, Art?"

He really did but refused to give in to that need. He knew it was just fear burning him inside, and the beer couldn't really put out that fire.

"I'm on duty, remember? One's the limit. A Chief is allowed just the one if the conditions warrant it."

"You're off the clock now," she said. "You're Art now. The Chief is taking a break."

He wanted to cry but was too afraid to. And he had to know that he could hold it together. He fought back the tears, though his eyes were seas of mist.

"I've killed people, Maggie. Twice."

Like pulling teeth, he thought, just to acknowledge it. It was a warm day, but that wasn't why he had begun to sweat. He felt a little sick. He wanted to lie down, but that wasn't an option.

"All told, I've been a cop twenty-five years. In two of those years, I shot people. Killed people."

He looked again at the porch floor.

"Art, you didn't have a choice, as I recollect it. I remember that deal, that fella you shot. I read it in the paper, heard folks talk. He tried to kill you. And he shot that boy. What was his name—that boy?"

Art looked up.

"Dom—Dominick." He had not thought of Dominick Cruikshank for some time. Maybe five years. Art managed a thin smile at the memory of him.

"He was just back from Vietnam, Maggie. A good kid trying to find his footing again."

"He survived, didn't he?"

"He did. Thank God for that."

Just visualizing Dom alive and well, somewhere out in Colorado, his life finally in order, made Art feel a little better, but not really by so much.

"Art, why'd that fella shoot him?"

Art reminded himself to be careful. There was more to that story than he could ever tell anyone. There was a secret that had to be guarded. Carolyn didn't know that secret. No one did except for Dominick. And one other person.

"Wrong place, wrong time," Art said. "It happens all the time. Dom got tangled up with this drug dealer drifting through town. Outside Bunnie's Tavern. There was a misunderstanding, a fight, and the guy shot Dom. People on collision courses. Fate, maybe."

"And so you had to shoot *him*," she said. "That's your job, unfortunately."

"He could have given up. He *should* have given up. He didn't have to die."

"When he shot at you, Art, he forfeited the right to live."

How many times had he told himself that one?

"That's easy enough for people to believe if they aren't doing the shooting." He felt a chill as it all came back to him. He could visualize clearly the dead man's face—Brant Russell, a nobody drug dealer from Indiana. But still, he had been a person. Someone's son.

Neither of them spoke for several minutes. Art's hands ached a little from gripping the railing so long. He crossed them across his chest and scooted along the railing where a column could support his back.

"What about this other one?" she said. "You said there were two shootings. I don't know about this other one."

Margo Townsend, he thought. A name attached to someone else he never knew and could never know. Another nobody, but someone's daughter. Another druggie, but someone who wasn't always an addict, wasn't always desperate enough to rob a store. Another person who fell off the map somehow and got themselves killed. Sad, sad, sad. Another person on a collision course.

"It was in Chicago, when I was a beat cop," Art said. "A woman robbed a convenience store. When I got there, she took a shot at me and I fired back, toward the muzzle flash. It was dark and in an alley behind the store. Dumb luck of a shot killed her. I think she got about two-hundred dollars. That's what she exchanged her life for—two hundred measly dollars."

Art ran a finger along the scar on his cheek.

"Goodness," Maggie said. She looked out over the fields. "You've damn sure been through the wars, Art."

He nodded sadly.

"I reckon I have."

After he left Maggie's, he started back to Argus but impulsively caught I-55 north to Chicago. Three hours later he was there, in that little South Side neighborhood, standing in that alley. He found the spot where he had stood when the bullet sought him out. The bushes he had fallen into were gone. The alley seemed much smaller than it had years before. He strolled the alley's length. It did all seem familiar, but quite distant, remote. More like a scene from a photograph he had seen than a place he really had inhabited. It was an alley from some old black and white movie.

The distance from where he had stood and where Margo fell seemed to be much longer than he remembered. That night it had seemed short. Maybe that was because it had been dark. And he had been terrified.

He looked up, at the window where a woman had screamed something after he shot Margo. He still could not recall what she had said. Her scream, though, was a faint echo in his head.

Art reached the spot where Margo had died. The shot had caught her hard frontally and ripped through her brain and exited the back. She might have been dead before she hit the ground. He hoped that was the case. He thought fleetingly of Brant Russell. He, too, had surely died very quickly. Another dead-on shot. Art couldn't claim to be a great shot, but in both cases, he had somehow been dead on.

Dead was the word all right.

Bullets and people.

Collision courses.

He studied where Margo had fallen: it was shitty soil, a little sandy with human debris mixed in. There were tiny pebbles, an empty Zippo lighter, some twisted washers, and a rusted penny. Art picked it up.

Finding a penny on the ground was good luck, he had always heard. He put it in his pocket and hoped that was true.

Art walked around the corner. The White Hen Pantry Margo had robbed wasn't there anymore. It was a café. Everything about the crime was gone—Margo, the store, the bushes where he had fallen. Time had marched on and had swept the ugly little incident away as it marched. He wondered whether there was anyone left in the neighborhood who remembered Margo. Did she still have family? Were there people inside that cafe who knew her, remembered her?

He went back for a last look down the alley. This time, from where Margo stood. He tried to imagine what went through her mind when he called for her to halt. She had not really hesitated. Instead, she had fired four times rapidly. Four explosions. He tried to picture his own muzzle flashes from where he stood. It was all over just like that. In a flash and an instant. No time to really think. He had felt the sting, returned fire, and she was down and gone forever.

He stood there a couple minutes, the event replaying in his head, but each time it seemed to be fading a little. The alley was quickly becoming just a place, a location from the past. He had begun to think the alley didn't look much at all like it did back then. He looked up again at the window where the woman had screamed. The window was painted over. It didn't look like anyone even lived there anymore. There was a Pepsi can on the ground and he kicked it, the can bouncing several times before rolling against the brick building.

Art looked once more along the length of the alley. He placed his hands on his hips and sighed heavily. Then he went back to the café and got coffee to go and walked down the street several blocks. There was someone he could talk to. With luck, he'd still be around.

He found Steve Parnell after some effort. The folks at Gil's Grill said he had stopped coming in for some time and was retired from the force. But someone knew where he lived over in Bridgeport, and Art knocked on the door of a small but well-maintained Victorian. Art saw that Steve didn't recognize him for a second or two when he opened the door.

"Shit," Steve finally said. "Who's this Barney Fucking Fife standing on my porch in his Eagle Scout uniform?"

"Yeah, yeah, yeah," Art said. "I've got your Barney Fife right here." He pretended to grab his crotch.

Steve stepped through the doorway and offered a meaty hand and they shook. Steve was a large man, perhaps six-two and two-fifty.

"That's some uniform you downstate honchos wear, Art. But where are the merit badges?"

"I donated them to the Smithsonian, ass wipe."

And then they hugged. Steve had been a good friend to Art when they had worked the turbulent South Side streets. Steve was the first to arrive the night Art shot Margo.

"You look about the same, Art."

"And you've packed on a pound or two, Stevie."

"Retirement," he said. "Been meaning to exercise more. It ain't like when we walked streets and lived on coffee. That kept us leaner."

"And meaner?"

"Something like that."

Awkward silence. The two men had not seen each other in fifteen years.

"When did you hang it up, Stevie?"

"Well, nearly two years ago. We came over to Bridgeport ten years ago. How do you like the house?"

"Damn spiffy," Art said. "How's Louise?"

"Doing great. Just fine. Still works at the hospital. I kid her that she can't retire for at least another ten years now that I'm in dry dock."

Art laughed.

"The Louise I remember probably had something to say about that."

"Oh, she did," Steve said. "Believe you me."

More silence. Steve punched Art lightly on the arm.

"Damn good to see you, Art. How'd you find me?"

"I stopped at Gil's, of course. "

"Good old Gil's. I stopped going there, though. There's a good tavern just a few blocks from here. That's where I watch the Bears now."

"Think they'll go all the way this year, Stevie?"

"Don't know. But I get this feeling it might be their best year ever. Fingers crossed."

"Then let's go see this new pub of yours," Art said. "I'll buy you a beer."

"And I'll drink it. But they might card you in that Girl Scout uniform."

Art smirked and shook his head. *Same old Stevie*, he thought.

"Maybe I can sell them some Girl Scout cookies."

The First Down Tavern was a true Bears den. Huge pictures of Dick Butkus, Walter Payton, Gale Sayers, and many others adorned the walls. A Bears banner was spread several yards on the wall behind the bar. The bartender, a thin, graying man, put two pints of Leinenkugel's in front of them on Bears coasters. He glanced a moment at Art's uniform, which certainly was out of place.

"I can only drink the one," Art said. "Still have to drive back to Argus."

"Hit and run, eh, Art?"

"Sorry, Stevie." Art sipped the beer. It was very cold and made his head hurt momentarily.

Steve nodded. "So, how's life down in Hooterville?"

"Argus."

"That's right—Mayberry," Steve said. He raised his pint. "To Argus, wherever the fuck that is."

"It's near Bloomington, Stevie. I'll get you a map."

"You do that."

They clinked the pints together and took hearty swigs.

"That's the coldest beer I ever tasted," Art said. "But it's good."

"Now you know why I come here."

"You come here because you only have to walk two blocks."

"Might have something to do with it," Steve said as he swiveled his stool toward Art. He squeezed Art's shoulder. "We go back a long way, Art. But no word from you in all this time? Is that right?"

Art shrugged.

"It may not be right, but it's accurate. I'm sorry, Stevie. You know what John Lennon said—life is what happens when you're making plans. Something like that."

"Jesus, Art. You show up after all these years and quote me John Lennon?"

"You want some Ditka quotes?"

"I might understand them."

Art looked down into his pint glass.

"Okay, okay. Look, I'm damn sorry. Once I left Chicago, it was almost like it didn't exist anymore. I needed out, and I got out. And I got plugged into my new life. I got married, I—"

"Married?" Steve's eyes were wide. "You finally got married? I'll be damned. When was this?"

"After my first year in Argus."

Steve stared at Art.

"And presumably you married a gal with a name?"

"Oh, shit. Yeah—Carolyn."

"I'll bet you don't deserve her."

He laughed and patted Art's back.

"That's probably true. She's great all right, Stevie. She's the one with the brains in the family."

"Family? Kids, too?"

"No, no kids." Art squirmed in his seat on that one. "We've been pretty busy. Carolyn teaches English at the high school. But we bought a house out on the lake, on Lake Argus."

Steve winked at Art.

"So you're a country squire now. In the yacht club, too?"

Art shook his head.

"C'mon, it's nothing like that. Not at all. It's a nice brick ranch. Good shade from the trees. Deer come into the backyard sometimes. And I've got a little boat and outboard tied up to the dock. But it ain't no yacht."

"Captain Millage," Steve said loudly. "I'm impressed." He raised his pint. "Here's to Captain Millage, commodore of the Lake Argus U-boat flotilla. Can you even swim, Art?"

"Learned in the Navy, dickhead." He looked Steve in the eyes. "Are we about done with Hooterville and Mayberry and Girl Scout uniforms, Stevie?"

Steve nodded, studied Art a moment warily.

"Sure. Whatever. But after all these years, though, maybe I get to jerk your chain some, don't you think?"

Art immediately felt bad for snarling. Steve was right.

"Yeah, I think you're entitled. I do apologize—sorry, old friend."

"Accepted." They shook firmly. "So, what else keeps you busy down in Argus?"

Art drained the rest of his beer and turned toward the bar and caught sight of himself in the mirror. He was surprised out how calm he appeared. As calmly as he could, Art said, "Oh, not so much—though I did have to kill someone again."

Steve looked at Art in the mirror. He swiveled back toward Art and rested an elbow on the bar. The bartender looked up from washing glasses at the far end and glanced at Steve expectantly, but Steve waved him off. Art was still staring at himself in the mirror.

"That's why you're here," Steve said flatly. "And you've been to that damn alley, too. I'd bet my ass and Mike Ditka on it."

Art finally leaned back from the bar and crossed his arms across his chest, but he still stared ahead into the mirror.

"I went by there a few hours ago when I hit town. Local tourist attraction and all that. Maybe they'll put out a plaque there, like on the North Side for the Valentine's Day Massacre."

Steve said quietly, "Did it do you any good to go there?"

Art glanced at him.

"Was it cathartic, do you mean?"

"Is that a John Lennon word, Art?"

"No, it's a word anyone can use. Even I know what it means."

Steve nodded, sipped his beer.

"I know what it means, too, Art."

After a while, Art said, "Wouldn't it be nice to just sit here all afternoon and drink cold beer? Cold Leinenkugel's beer. And talk about the Bears and the Cubs. I haven't done anything like that in years. Literally years."

Steve waved the bartender over.

"Frankie, Chief Millage here needs to use your phone. Official downstate police business."

Frankie brought the phone and sat it on the bar in front of Art.

"Call your wife, Art. Call—Carolyn. Tell her you're up here for the night. Then call your office and tell whoever your best man is to take over until you get back tomorrow. You hearing me, Art?"

Art nodded slowly. He reached for the phone.

"Yeah, I hear you, Stevie. Thanks."

They had gotten drunk at the tavern and stayed on late into the night and Art told the story of Brant Russell. When they staggered back to Steve's house, Louise supplied them with blankets and pillows for the downstairs sofas. They didn't even wake up when she left for work early the next morning. By almost noon, they had managed to make some coffee and Art had showered before slipping back into his wrinkled uniform. They walked back down to The First Down for some lunch—rare roast beef, the tavern specialty. Then Steve had Art drive them over to the alley where he had shot Margo.

"Since you went to all this trouble, you might as well see the place for what it really is," Steve said.

Art looked down the alley and then at Steve.

"I'm listening. What is it really?"

"Just a damn alley, man. Nothing more. Not even a particularly scenic or interesting one. I can take you to alleys that have character, history. I could show you one where Al Capone had a little office. This is just a sawed-off little bastard of an alley that starts at nowhere and ends at nowhere."

"Tell that to Margo Townsend, Stevie. She knows about being nowhere."

"She tried to kill you," Steve said. "She packed a forty-five, brother—not some twenty-two pea shooter. She carried heavy artillery to make sure she got what she shot at."

Art touched his cheek, the scar.

"And she almost did. Another inch or so the other way and I'm the sack of potatoes getting loaded into the meat wagon."

Steve walked a few paces down the alley and looked up along the brick walls a moment. He turned back toward Art.

"I know she was a person. I get that. She had a momma and a daddy and all that. But she was also a corked-out junkie lugging a cannon of a firearm, and she didn't think twice about trying to waste you if it meant getting what she wanted. Your life for hers is a lousy trade. Sometimes a person needs to be shot for what they do. That don't make it pleasant, but sometimes it just has to be."

Art nodded.

"I guess I know that. I guess I see that—now, finally. Maybe I had to come here again to put her to rest. That's starting to make sense."

"And that takes us to door number two," Steve said. "This other one—Brant Russell."

A jumbled set of images of the dead Brant Russell cascaded in Art's head and he felt queasy.

"I thought *he* was dead and buried, too, all these years. Stevie, all of a sudden, years later, I'm walking around with two ghosts following me."

"Don't see them that way, Art."

"What are they if they aren't ghosts?"

"Events. Life is full of events. Period."

"Events. That's rich, Stevie. They didn't die, they had events. They died from an event."

"Life ain't perfect," Steve said. "Far from it. We move constantly between good and bad, and in between we carve out an existence, a life. Tomorrow isn't guaranteed and yesterday can't be done over."

Art wanted to laugh but avoided it.

"Did you read that in a book?"

Steve smiled.

"No. But after I retired I went to a shrink for a few months. I was damn skeptical at first, but Louise suggested it. She said I might get some good out of talking with someone about things coming to an end—being a cop. I did it more than forty years, Art."

"And it worked?"

"Yeah. Yeah, it did. I decompressed, I guess. How's that for a big Lennon word? But it made it easier to close the door on being a cop. I talked my way through the transition. Sounds to me like you never decompressed, Art."

"I thought leaving Chicago for Argus would do that. I hoped, anyway."

"And maybe it would have, if there hadn't been Brant Russell. But he came along and you had to do it again, and then you had two of them on your hands. Then it was just a matter of time. You've been a ticking time bomb."

"Or maybe a long-buried bullet finally working its way to the surface."

Steve shrugged.

"That works, too."

Art looked up and down the alley. He had begun to really see it as only an empty alley. Well, almost. He looked at Steve.

"Now what?"

"Now you go home. You drive back to that little town of yours and sit down with your wife, and you tell her all the things you haven't told her about this."

"And after that?"

"After that you live your life, Art. You do the best you can every day and try not to look back because you can't change the past. You get over the past."

After a few moments Art said, "Give me a minute, Stevie."

"Sure. Take your time."

Steve went back to the car, looking back once.

Art stood over the spot where Margo Townsend died—where he'd killed her. It was an event all right. He could still picture her sprawled dead on the ground but had to admit the image was fading—slightly.

"I'm sorry, Margo. Really, I am. Jesus. I sure wish I could undo it, but I can't. I don't really know what else to say except I hope you find peace. I'm going to look for it, too."

He stared at the ground a moment and then he drove Steve home and said his goodbyes and headed south to Argus. When he reached Lake Argus, the last rays of the sun were streaming west.

Summer

Seven

By July, Art still had not told Carolyn anything more about Margo Townsend than she already knew, which wasn't much. He had also begun to go to work later, often not rising until after she had left for school. And one morning he decided not to wear his uniform to work. There was no rule against it that he knew of and so he selected olive-drab, pleated slacks and a crisp, white oxford shirt with a button-down collar. He'd always liked how a button-down collar framed his neck and chin.

In the mirror, he saw it was time for a haircut. He studied his hair, still brown and thick with a side part and a smidgen of gray at each temple. The gray was so subtle that he realized slightly longer hair on the sides would hide it. He made a mental note to skip the haircut and see how that turned out.

On the way into Argus, he drove by Maggie Thomas's house but didn't stop. He was tempted but resisted it. He wasn't sure why. When he got to town, instead of going to the station, he aimlessly cruised neighborhoods for half an hour, just looking at houses and waving sometimes to people on sidewalks. Art enjoyed gazing at the towering old Victorians. The beauty of drifting in a police car, Art noted, was that no one would suspect you were drifting. It was as though the real Art was someplace else while the cardboard cutout Art cruised neighborhoods or walked streets, stopping to nod and chat—looking and acting like The Chief. Projecting Chief.

In addition to his clothes, his young deputies, Red, Scotty Simms, and Bill Gaines, also noticed that Art wasn't wearing his gun that morning. They convened in the coffee room to discuss it, and Art figured he'd better head off the discussion.

"Morning, boys," Art said. He poured himself some coffee and had a sip. "I see Red made the coffee this morning." He pretended to make a sour face. "It's sure thick and strong."

They watched him take a second sip. Art attempted humor and a smile.

"Red, any calls from Maggie Thomas this morning?"

That at least got a grin from Red.

"Nothing yet, Chief. But it's early for her. You know Maggie."

"Indeed, I do."

Art thought, *Far more than you ever will, my young friend.*

Bill said, "Chief, are you going someplace?"

"Just back to my desk, Bill. Why do you ask?"

"You're not in uniform."

Art nodded, sipped more coffee.

"You're sharp, Bill. You *should* be a detective."

Art saw that Bill looked surprised and a little hurt and he reminded himself to smooth that over later.

"Chief, did you forget your gun?" Red said.

"No. It's in my briefcase, on my desk."

"You're not going to wear it?"

"You know I don't wear it around the office."

"Yeah, but you always come to work wearing it." Red hesitated, and then added, "When you wore your uniform, that is."

"Maybe it's time for a change," Art said. "Can't I still be Chief in a white shirt and no gun?"

The three deputies looked at each other, Art thought, as though it was a trick question, or an algebra equation beyond their grasp. Take away the guns and uniforms, Art thought, and they really could be just overgrown high school boys debating whether to go shoot hoops at the park or check out girls at the drug store. Both sounded like more palatable options to Art than working.

"I'll be in my office, boys."

He felt their eyes on his back all the way down the hall.

Art spent the rest of the morning in his office doing almost nothing. He had to field a call from the State Police, but it was a routine matter. There were some papers to sign, and he managed to focus long enough to understand what he was signing and approving. Minor stuff. He'd not remember much of it by lunch.

By noon, he decided to surprise Carolyn and take her to lunch. The notion had popped unexpectedly into his head. He hadn't done that in quite some time. He wondered why but couldn't come up with an answer.

As he headed out the door, Red called after him, "Chief, you're forgetting your gun."

Art stopped and instinctively patted the hip where it usually lived. He smiled and tossed Red a very sloppy salute.

"I'm not forgetting a thing."

Art and Carolyn ate pizza at Monical's across the street from the high school. She had been quite surprised to see him show up out of uniform. They were still talking about it when they reached Monical's and sat in a booth near the door. Art noticed that several people, including the young waitress, also seemed to take note that he was out of uniform.

"It's just that I'm so used to seeing you in uniform away from home," Carolyn said.

He thought she looked very sexy in heels and a snug blue dress that offered a hint of cleavage. He could smell her perfume but elected not to say so because he wasn't sure what it was called. He was very sure that if he brought it up, he *should* be able to name it. He could imagine high school boys getting boners in her classes.

Boners, he thought. *What a funny word.*

"You haven't said how I look, though," Art said. He thought again, fleetingly, about letting his hair grow a little longer.

She smiled.

"Sharp, of course. You look crisp as lettuce at the store in that button-down shirt."

She reached over and squeezed his hand, and it sent a tiny chill. Their marriage still produced such things, and he was glad for it.

"But I see you like this when we go out," she said. "It's just that nobody sees you around town by day unless you're in uniform—being the Chief."

"Sometimes I need a break from being the costumed crusader," he said, "and need a break from being Chief."

"My, my," she said. "What got poured into *your* coffee this morning?"

"Red made it today. It's high octane."

"I guess so. Next, you'll rip open your shirt and beat your chest like Tarzan."

"Should I?"

He grinned broadly and undid a shirt button.

She actually blushed, and he was pleased.

"I don't think Argus is ready for the Chief to become Tarzan and ravish women at Monical's," she said. "Save that for when we get home."

"I'll do just that."

"Then call me Jane," she said, and they both laughed loud enough that people looked their way.

Eight

After a few weeks, the people of Argus were used to seeing Art out of uniform, though he had heard that the City Council had made it an agenda item for a meeting in a few weeks. He wasn't worried about that. The council was mostly a gaggle of well-meaning but quite spineless folks who never agreed on much of substance. And he still had a longstanding chit he could cash in on Mayor Sullivan. It had a lot to do with the mayor banging someone not his wife. The mayor in turn had various chits on council members, and the bottom line was that if the mayor played ball for Art, the council would play ball for Art, too.

No one had a chit on Art. He was fairly sure.

Instead of worrying about it, Art had driven over to Bloomington-Normal and bought more oxford shirts and new slacks and even new shoes, too, at Bergner's. As far as Art was concerned, the Chief uniform was retired. It no longer suited him. It was a costume. He reminded himself to call Stevie and tell him. That would no doubt produce a couple pretty good wisecracks.

Back in Argus, he walked along Main Street and looked in store windows. Fleener Hardware had a new riding lawn mower in their window, and Art stopped to look. They had a good-sized yard out at the lake. He wondered whether he needed such a monstrosity. It was the sort of machine used by people serious about their grass. So serious, Art felt, that it bordered on obsession. *What did grass do before there were mowers,* he mused. *A funny question. How did nature ever get along without people to tame it, humiliate it, and convert it?*

It was a day for funny thoughts, he concluded. Not hot, but sunny and bright. He filed the riding mower away for future reference. For now, he would keep paying the neighborhood kid to mow. It gave the boy something to do and a few bucks.

As he strolled, he saw Roger Gilstrap, owner of Gilstrap's Texaco, coming out of Cameron's Café. He was a burly man, still given to wearing long and rather bushy sideburns that always made Art think of that odd-looking Civil War general—Burnside. Ambrose Burnside. What a name. Roger, like Art, was defined by a uniform—a green Texaco uniform with his name stenciled over a breast pocket.

Art could not recall ever seeing Roger out of uniform and wondered what he might be like in his private life. Or was he one of those men who went from day uniform to night uniform, as many did, exchanging work clothes for essentially cleaner work clothes at home. It was as though some men would feel naked or exposed if not in some sort of uniform, if not conforming to something larger than themselves that gave them comfort and an ironic sense of identity in the anonymity.

Some men, he knew, identified solely with their job, and going home was an uneasy alliance with a wife and time not working. It was a place they didn't feel fully comfortable at. A place where they sometimes did not quite know what to do with themselves—so they mowed lawns obsessively and tinkered with things that didn't need to be fixed. They were like soldiers between battles sitting around in quiet boredom, waiting for something to happen.

"Hi, Roger. Late breakfast?"

Roger had to do a double take. Art was learning there was still an adjustment of sorts for some folks to seeing The Chief dressed like a citizen.

"Hey, Chief. Didn't see it was you right off."

"Call me Art. After all, I've known you about fifteen years."

"Okay, Chief–Art."

They shook hands. Roger had a strong grip and massive hands. Art's hand nearly disappeared in the grip. The Texaco station was two blocks in the direction Art was headed and he offered to walk with Roger.

"How's business, Roger?"

"It ain't half bad."

Art nodded, knew Roger was one of those men of very few words, who were laconic because they preferred being busy and working to chatting. For them, often language was just a necessity to get someplace or get something done. Another tool in their toolbox, but not their favorite one. It was the one they knew the least about and felt least comfortable using.

"What's gas up to now?" Art said.

"A buck and twenty, Art."

Art realized it was something he really didn't know. The deputies always took care of gassing his car. A perk. Maybe a silly one at that. Was he a prince? He decided to start filling up the car himself.

"Really? That much?"

"I can remember when it was thirty-five cents," Roger said.

"When was that?"

"Back in 1970."

"Really?" His first year in Argus was 1970. The year he met Carolyn. The year of Dominick Cruikshank and a wispy drug dealer named Jesse Archer.

And the year of Brant Russell.

And only two years after the year of Margo Townsend.

Art was remembering it all when they reached the Texaco station in silence.

Roger said, "Art, how come you don't wear the uniform no more?"

Art plunged his hands into his pants pockets. He looked down the street, where it disappeared around a curve and became the road to Lake Argus—to his house.

"I don't need it anymore. Everybody knows by now who I am."

Roger shrugged.

"I guess that's so. Can't deny it. But the gun? I see you don't wear that no more, either."

"Guns scare people."

It wasn't the answer Art had hoped for.

"Sure they do. But they're handy when the time comes."

"The deputies are well-armed. And on the job, Roger."

Art sensed the not-so-subtle reproach and didn't much care for it.

"But they ain't the Chief," Roger said.

"No, they're not."

"They've never had to use their guns," Roger said.

"No, they haven't."

"You have."

"Yes. I have."

Roger rubbed one of his long sideburns.

"You ever think much on that—Art?"

"No," Art lied. "Not much. The past is past. You ever think much about thirty-five cent gas—Roger?"

Roger smirked.

"Not so much. The past is past—right?"

"That's right, Roger."

They stared at each other a long moment.

"Well, I got to get back to it, Chief—Art."

"You take care, Roger."

Art watched Roger walk to one of the service bays where a truck was on a lift. He watched as Roger pointed out something under the truck to the kid mechanic. Then Art walked further down the street, several times absently reaching for the vacant spot on his hip where he used to wear his weapon.

Nine

Art had taken to walking the streets of Argus every day. It was as though he had become a beat cop again, like back in Chicago. He checked into the station first thing of a morning and had coffee with the deputies, then set off for downtown and walked. He had even lost a couple pounds and felt—friskier.

On this day, he had made his circuit around the courthouse square and had even walked down a few side streets into neighborhoods. Back at the square, he refreshed his coffee at Cameron's and sat on a bench for a minute. Across the street he eyed a new business, a hair salon—Le Salon. He knew that meant The Salon. He had seen places like it in Chicago, on the North Side. They could be sort of arrogant establishments, but pleasant enough once you peeked inside and smelled all the different scents from perfume and hair products. Le Salon would be a greatly watered -down version of the Chicago salons, he suspected.

Doris Pearcy, a friend of Carolyn's who ran a florist shop next to Cameron's, came out of Le Salon, poking and tugging at her hair, which was still a little wet, Art noticed. She was a fortyish blonde (with some chemical help), still attractive, and married to the county clerk. After a moment, she appeared satisfied with things and crossed the street.

"Holding down that bench, are you, Art?" she said.

"That's right, Doris. It ain't going anywhere."

"Looks like you're doing a crackerjack job of it."

Art knew how the game was played.

"Doing my best, Doris."

"Well, you keep at it, Art."

"On the job, Doris."

She smiled and waved and headed back to her shop. Art glanced once as she went through the door, still fussing a bit with her hair.

Lanky Ike Lassitter walked by and waved to Art. Ike tended bar at the VFW and did odd jobs around town, too.

"Taking her easy, Art?"

"Easy as I can, Ike. How about you?"

"Taking it any way I can," Ike said.

"There you go, Ike."

"Have a good one, Chief." Ike headed on down toward the VFW on the corner.

"I'll do that," Art said to Ike's back.

Art chuckled about the art of conversation in Argus. A lot seemed to get said, but little amounted to much. He knew there was a sort of tradition of always greeting each other on the street with meaningless statements. On the surface, it could all seem innocent enough, but he felt there was a darker side to it: when the chips were down, how many of these good citizens would really step up and be there for a neighbor when it mattered? He suspected not so many. That was his job, after all.

Most people wanted to just sail along every day, unimpeded, and go to their jobs and then go home and in between issue fake smiles and say, "Have a nice day, take it easy, don't work too hard, how's it going, how's it hanging, how's your day going so far, how's the family, what are you up to, think it'll rain, don't take any wooden nickels, see you later, see you soon, see you around, take care."

He finished his coffee and tossed the cup into a trashcan under the Cameron's awning. Looking up, he caught sight of himself in the window and noticed his hair had finally grown out some. He ran fingers through the sides, and then remembered to look around to see if anyone was watching. The sidewalk was empty, and he relaxed, dug his hands into his pockets, and surveyed the square a moment. He could head back to the station now, his morning regime done. There would be some paperwork to oversee. The deputies would report in from patrol—but there would be nothing to report, of course.

Instead, Art stepped across the street and entered Le Salon. Inside it was brighter than Art had anticipated. He needed a moment for his eyes to adjust and felt rather like he had suddenly walked onstage at a theater. He could hear water running and saw a young redheaded woman in a blue smock giving another young woman a shampoo. There were several more women of varying ages reading ladies magazines in a little waiting area by the door, and a girl who looked barely eighteen behind the reception counter. She was scribbling something in an appointment book spread open on the counter. The ladies reading magazines seemed awfully intent on their reading. Art didn't recognize any of them. He could smell shampoo and the conversations at various styling chairs around the room were low and he could not immediately make out words and sentences.

He nearly turned to leave, but the receptionist looked up and smiled. She had an angelic face, blue eyes, and her blonde hair was piled on her head in such a way that Art wondered what kept it from falling.

"Yes, sir," she said. "Do you have an appointment?"

Art was glad no one seemed to know who he was.

"No." He hesitated. "Do I need one?"

"Not at all," she said, studying the appointment book. "It looks like Sabrina has time right now."

"Oh," was all Art could say momentarily. He wasn't sure he really had meant to get a haircut.

"Why don't you have a seat, sir, and I'll see if she's ready."

The girl disappeared around a corner and Art sat in a chair by the window. He picked through the magazines on a table— mostly magazines about hair and women's fashion—but nothing interested him. The girl returned, smiling. She was followed by a woman in a blue smock who looked to be in her early thirties with pale skin and very dark hair down on her shoulders and a few curls here and there. Like all the other women in the salon, Art did not know her. Who were all these strangers in his town?

"I'm Sabrina."

She wore a lot of dark eye shadow. Art felt the name fit her, too.

"Art." Then he remembered to stand and offer a hand. It was one of those handshakes, he noted, that was mighty brief and elusive. He knew that some women just never felt comfortable doing it.

She studied his hair a moment, placed her hands on her hips, and cocked her head.

"So, what are we doing today," she said.

Art needed a couple seconds before he understood what she meant.

"Oh," he said, looking away for a second, "I guess I need a haircut."

She frowned slightly.

"You're not sure?" But then she smiled. "Why don't you come back to my chair and we'll have a look. That okay, Art?"

He looked around the salon.

"Sure. Let's have a look—Sabrina."

She sat him in the swiveling chair and faced him toward the mirror and immediately ran fingers through his hair on the sides.

"You're getting some weight here," she said.

Art wasn't completely sure of the implications of that but nodded.

"So, what's the plan?" she said. "Have you always had this side part?"

Art stared at himself in the mirror. It was disconcerting to do so with another face hovering above him.

"I have," he said. "Why do you ask?" He studied it in the mirror. He noticed the sides had grown just enough to hide the gray flecks at his temples. He also thought humor might help.

"Is a side part just not hip anymore?" He managed a weak smile, saw it was a bit lopsided in the mirror.

She seemed to study him intently in the mirror.

"It's okay. Conservative, but okay. Have you considered a middle part?"

"Down the middle?" Art had images of oily hair with middle parts from the 1920s or 1930s. Men wearing straw skimmer hats. That always seemed a bit funny looking to him.

"Isn't that a sort of old-fashioned, the slicked down look?" he said.

She nodded, seemed to inspect a section of his hair.

"We wouldn't slick it down, Art. And it wouldn't be a definite part—more like just cutting it so the hair lies well on each side and then falls a little forward."

"Bangs?" Art didn't think bangs were in the cards for him. "Like the Beatles?"

She laughed softly.

"Don't worry, you won't look like the Beatles."

"Maybe," he said, still pondering it, trying to visualize it. He liked The Beatles but didn't want to try to look like them.

"And we keep this side length, too," she said.

He nodded. "I'd been thinking of that, yes." The way she described it, it didn't sound bad at all. "Okay, Sabrina. Let's do it."

"That's the spirit, Art. We'll have you living in the current decade in no time at all."

He frowned.

"Was I so out of style?"

She rested her hands on his shoulders and squeezed gently to reassure him.

"No, no—not at all. That's not really what I meant. You looked fine. Conservative, but fine. But you're a youthful-looking man. This new style will accentuate that."

Sabrina guided him to a chair and sink in another room and helped him into a smock, which made Art feel ridiculous. It was nearly as bad as one of those things they made you wear in a hospital that left your butt sticking out. What would the deputies think if they saw him? How about Carolyn?

But he kept his mouth shut and leaned back in the chair, and she checked the temperature of the water before washing his hair. She did it slowly, and Art thought it felt very good. The water was warm but not hot. He could not recall a woman ever shampooing his hair before. He closed his eyes and relaxed. It was much more of an intimate experience than he ever imagined it would be. It seemed faintly—sexual. Or perhaps he meant sensual. Either way, it was very relaxing, and he felt he could easily fall into a nap, and for a long and luxurious moment, he did nap while Sabrina applied conditioner lovingly, slowly, working it into the hair and then washing it out.

Ten

Sabrina had put something in his hair that made it stand up too much and Art felt self-conscious. So much so that he called the station and told Red he was going home for the day. There he changed into shorts, t-shirt, and tennis shoes and walked down to the dock and fired up the little motorboat. It was light and powered by a seventy-five horse Evinrude outboard and it could scoot. He cruised slowly out of the bay, and when he reached the main channel of the lake, he gunned the throttle and the bow rose and then fell with a splash, and the propeller dug in, and the boat sped south toward the dam.

Art stood up, his right hand on the wheel, and allowed the wind and spray off the lake to thoroughly scour his hair. He ran his fingers through it when it was good and wet. At the dam. he made a lazy turn and throttled back and motored slowly along shore, headed back north. Halfway back to his own bay, he entered a bay without houses along its shore and cut the engine and allowed the boat to drift along the shore. He retrieved an Eagle Claw spinning rod from under one of the gunwales and attached a Garcia Mitchell open-face reel to it. The reel had been kept dry in a compartment of the boat's dashboard. Art ran a line from the reel's bale up through the eyelets and then attached a Mepps spinner from a tackle box in the other gunwale.

As the boat slowly drifted and water lapped against the hull, Art cast the spinner toward a submerged tree stump and retrieved it slowly. He enjoyed the motions of casting a lure. It was not so different to him than throwing a baseball in terms of repetitive motions and rhythm—and pleasure. Art enjoyed the sound made as the line was stripped from the reel's bale each time he cast the spinner. It was a rather high-pitched hissing sound. He enjoyed the arc and trajectory of the spinner as it was launched from the rod until it plopped into the water.

Art did not care whether he caught any fish. That wasn't necessary. He was not a regular fisherman. But he enjoyed being on the water and the exercise of casting and the accuracy he developed at placing the spinner near a stump or among reeds against the shore.

He enjoyed casting for half an hour and then he dropped the anchor and opened the passenger seat into a recliner and lay down, the waves gently rocking the boat until he fell asleep.

He woke up hours later, and a light rain began to fall. He felt refreshed from the nap and enjoyed the clean smell of the rain and how it made millions of drops and circles on the surface of the bay. He watched that process for several minutes, rain dripping down his forehead, before raising anchor and firing up the outboard. His clothes were soaked, but he did not mind, and it was not cold. At the mouth to the bay, he stood up and plunged the throttle and the rush of wind dried out his hair and he stood all the way up the lake to the mouth of his own bay.

At home, he toweled dry and changed into jeans and a t-shirt and poured himself a tumbler of Laphroaig scotch on the rocks with a splash of water and sat in a chair out by the dock. The surface of the lake was as smooth as glass. He could feel his hair fall slightly on his forehead and he instinctively brushed it back. It had looked fine in the bedroom mirror, though. Sabrina had been right: it wasn't really bangs and instead just the hair falling forward some instead of swept back and Art honestly felt he looked better, younger.

The scotch tasted strongly of peat, and he enjoyed the taste and smell. Ducks floated noisily out on the bay, but Art had always liked the sound of ducks. They seemed so happy, so oblivious to everything. Rain or shine, ducks sailed along merrily. He watched them a while and then remembered Carolyn would be home very soon. He was getting hungry. He finished the scotch and let the warmth from it soak in and envelop him like a warm blanket. Soon he heard her car pull into the driveway.

There was a small diner across the lake at the marina. Carolyn had changed into shorts and a t-shirt, too, and they set off into the lake slowly, both carrying scotches, Art laughing that they were very much like lake gentry with time to enjoy.

"I can't get over your hair, Art." Carolyn ran her fingers through it. "You actually went to that new salon. I've been meaning to check it out, too."

Art sipped his scotch. He had a nice buzz.

"Well, if you do, ask for Sabrina."

"Oh? Was she very young and pretty?" Carolyn had rested her hand on the back of his neck.

Art pondered the question.

"More like thirties and rather pale."

After a few seconds, he added, "And no one there seemed to know me. I liked that."

She sipped scotch and laughed abruptly.

"Goodness. With the uniform retired and a new haircut, you're becoming the invisible Chief."

He wondered whether that could be true.

"So, you like the new cut?"

He glanced over at her.

She ran her hand across the top of his head.

"It's spiffy. You're like a new man."

He ran his hand along the inside of her bare thigh.

"How about a date, then, with a new man?"

"The throttle's in your hands, baby," she said.

"That ain't all," Art said as he pushed the throttle full forward and they plowed through waves toward the marina.

After dinner, they cruised south toward the dam, Carolyn at the helm, the moon out and making the water ahead of them sparkle. Art had drunk a couple beers with dinner and with his scotch foundation, he was slightly drunk. They had a couple beers with them, and Carolyn cut the engine along the shore. They sipped the beers and drifted.

"The conservation warden wouldn't be impressed if he saw me drinking out here on the lake," Art said. "And no running lights, either."

"We're being wicked," Carolyn said.

"Here's to it," Art said, and they clinked the bottles together. "Besides, that old warden never comes out at night. He's home safe in his bed."

Carolyn pinched Art's arm lightly.

"Will I be safe when we get home to *our* bed?"

"Not a bit, babe."

"Good answer," she said. "I'll hold you to it."

"You can hold it as long as you like."

She slapped his thigh playfully.

"The Chief sounds awfully frisky," she said.

"The Chief will have to wait. You're dealing with Art now—Art and his new haircut."

She ran her hand through his hair and tousled it thoroughly.

"Sounds like a threesome to me," she said, and they both laughed loudly.

Art felt blessed to have Carolyn, his house, his little boat—his life. It was a well-managed marriage, based on mutual respect. They had few secrets, but did have one, and Art decided it was time to air it out. He had sat on it for too many years.

"Carol, do you ever think about Dominick and Jesse?"

"Now there are two names from long ago," she said. "How long has it been since you saw them?"

"Back in seventy-five. Ten years. But they were both doing well, had their lives back on track."

"Thank God," she said. "I can still imagine Dom lying in the lot at Bunnie's, bleeding—and you off after that other boy."

"Brant Russell."

It no longer stung quite as much to say the name, Art noticed. It was now just a name. That's what fifteen years could finally accomplish, he supposed.

"Yes, Brant Russell," she said. "Do you still see his face sometimes?"

"Sure. I always will, I guess. Part of the deal."

She put both arms around him and leaned into his shoulder.

"We don't have to talk about it. Not really. Not at all. That's over. That's been over a long time."

Art was tempted to go along but couldn't quite do it.

"Actually, there is something, Carol. Something you should know."

"Oh?" she said. She rose up. "What did I miss?"

He leaned back and looked up at the moon.

"You know the basics, but not the essentials," he said, regretting how cryptic it sounded.

"I teach English, Art, but I have no idea what that means."

"Sorry, babe. Look, here's the deal—you know what Jesse was about. He dealt dope. He was small time, but—"

"But he got involved in some big deal and it went sour," she said. "And you had to stop that Brant Russell. He shot at you. I was there, remember?"

"That's right. And poor Dom was just caught in the middle. Literally standing in the wrong place at the wrong time and he got shot. He could have been killed."

She shrugged.

"So, where's the mystery?"

He hesitated, saw himself, back in that time, having that talk with Dom and Jesse after Dom had recovered and Brant Russell had long been shipped back to Indiana for burial.

"It's the money, Carol. That's what you don't know."

He wondered how she would judge him on it.

She stared at him. There was enough moonlight that he could see her face well.

"The money from the dealer—from Brant Russell," she said flatly. "I know about that. You gave it to the city."

Art finished his beer. It had gotten warm.

"*Some* of it."

He could see her eyebrows arch.

"Some of it?"

"Five grand of it, anyway."

"How much was there?"

"A lot more than that."

He tried to smile but knew he was making a mess of it.

She sagged back in her seat.

"How much more?"

"Another twenty-five grand."

"Jesus, Art. Where did it go?"

"I gave it to Dom and Jesse. I split it between them."

"Did you keep any?"

"Not a dime."

She looked puzzled.

"And the five thousand you gave the town, that was—"

"Symbolic," Art said, rather proud of his choice of word.

"And cover," she said.

"That, too. Can't deny it."

After a pause, Carolyn sighed and said, "Wow. Good Lord."

"He didn't get a cut," Art said, hoping humor would help.

"I guess I'm wondering why you haven't told me this after years all these years, Art."

He didn't think she sounded angry. And then he remembered what often was said in movies and realized it was also true enough in this case.

"Plausible deniability. To keep you out of it, in case it ever became something."

She nodded. He knew the gears were turning in her head. She was pretty analytical.

"And why did you split it between Dom and Jesse?"

That, at least, was still clear enough after all the years.

"Those two boys needed a direction. They were ready for it. So, I financed it."

"You took the law into your own hands," she said. "You defined it, interpreted it."

"Hell, I ignored it, Carolyn. And I didn't take that decision lightly at the time, either. I still don't."

She put her empty bottle in a cup holder. Art watched her closely.

"You weren't tempted to keep any of the money?" she said.

Art didn't like how that even sounded.

"No. I'm not built that way, Carolyn."

She patted his thigh.

"I know that, Art. But I had to ask. I know you're about as honest as the day is long."

"But I did break the law."

"How do you feel about that?"

He looked out over the calm surface of the lake, the moon reflected and shimmering.

"I still feel good about it, to tell you the truth. Sometimes the letter of the law doesn't cover it. Sometimes going by the book leaves someone out. It was an opportunity to convert Brant Russell's evil into good, and I took it. That's a speech, I guess. But it's how I see it."

Her hand in his, clasping his tightly, was all he needed to know.

Eleven

The summer had begun cool, warmed up a few weeks, but abruptly dropped back into cool with rain as light as mist for a few days. People reported that the fish had stopped biting for a while out on Lake Argus. It seemed more like early spring than July, and the atmosphere struck some as having an electric charge. Some folks even became irritable. There were more fights at Bunnie's Tavern one Friday night than people could ever recall.

Art chalked it all up to the weather, though Red said it had something to do with ionization. Red had read that in a book.

"I didn't even know you could read," Art said, but smiling.

"Good one, Chief."

"Can't you just call me Art? We're not the LAPD, you know. This is Mayberry. Relax. Accept it. And sit on this bench for crying out loud."

Red sat, but didn't appear comfortable at it, Art noted. They were sitting across from Cameron's.

"I should call you Chief in public, Chief."

"Suit yourself. What's this ionization business about?"

"The air can be ionized. That can make it rain."

Art nodded. He was impressed that Red had expanded his reading beyond the sports page of the *Pantagraph*.

"And I'm going to assume that ions are involved in all this, Red?"

"That's correct. It's all about electrons and atoms and such. I'm still sifting through it."

"Let me know how it comes out," Art said.

"You'll be the first, Chief."

Art nodded.

"And you read about all this where? Terry's Barbershop, maybe?"

"At the library."

Red was chock full of surprises, he thought.

"Not much crime at a library, though I do hear they need help tracking down overdue books. Red, maybe there's a career for you as a book bounty hunter."

"Another good one, Chief. Actually, I heard about some stranger hanging out over there. I went to check it out. While I was waiting, I read about ionization."

"Logical," Art said, hoping that Red could improve at catching the subtle hints of leg-pulling. "Something on your mind, Red?"

"Well, the stranger didn't show, but Mrs. Oliver at the circulation desk said he had been in a few times. She didn't know him."

"Did Mrs. Oliver know *you*, seeing how you never used to spend much time at the library?"

"The uniform was a dead giveaway, Chief."

"You got me there."

"You like to josh with me, don't you, Chief?"

"I guess I do. It builds character. And I wouldn't bother if I didn't like you."

"Okay. That's good to know. Can I ever josh with you, Chief?"

"Sure. But just at the station, I suppose. Appearances and all that."

"Got it, Chief. Only at the station."

"I'm kidding. Josh me any time you want. Now tell me more about this stranger."

"I've never seen him, Chief."

Art was already starting to think about lunch at the VFW. Maybe the roast beef. Or the Italian beef, with those lovely little green peppers.

"He sounds like an apparition of sorts, Red. Maybe he's in town to fish out on the lake. And he hits the library while it rains. Been raining a lot the last few days."

Art looked up at the sky, which was cloudy and held the promise of rain.

"I don't think so, Chief. This guy asked Mrs. Oliver to help him run the microfiche machine to look at old copies of the newspaper."

"Did Mrs. Oliver say what this mysterious stranger is interested in?"

"Yeah, she did. She said he wanted to read about you and what happened to Brant Russell all those years ago."

Art felt like someone has slapped the back of his head, but to Red he maintained outward calm and looked straight ahead. To appear nonchalant, he silently counted to ten before replying.

"Well, I wouldn't read much into it. Anyone can go over there and run that rickety little machine and read about it."

It occurred to Art that he never had.

"Mrs. Oliver said she couldn't recall the last time anyone did, though," Red said.

Still trying his best to seem disinterested, Art said, "Did she describe this stranger?"

Red pulled a pad from his breast pocket and read from it.

"Mid-twenties, brown hair, scraggly beard. About five-ten. She wasn't sure about weight, but said he was sort of stocky. He wore jeans and a light blue windbreaker over a white t-shirt that last day she saw him—a couple days ago."

After a long moment Art said, "Did she get a name?"

"No, no name that she recalled. She helped him load the fiche, and that was pretty much it."

Art nodded.

"That's a good report. Solid cop work."

"Thanks, Chief."

Art thought Red looked at him as though awaiting orders for battle.

"Is there something more?"

"Well, yeah. I mean, you have to admit it's mysterious."

Art shrugged, looked back over at Cameron's.

"What's so mysterious?"

"Chief, he's poking around about that shooting. He's snooping into—you."

"It's a free country. They make back issues of the paper available so folks can have a look. Maybe he's a history buff."

Art stood up and Red stuffed the pad back in the pocket and got up, too.

"But, Chief—he don't seem like anyone from around here."

"You know that for a fact?"

Red frowned.

"No, I don't. But Mrs. Oliver said she's never seen him at the library before."

"Mrs. Oliver lives in Bloomington and goes back there every day at five or so, Red. She doesn't know half this town and sees only the folks who show up at her desk. If Hitler lived here, she wouldn't know it unless he tried to check out *Mein Kampf*."

"Good point, Chief. That's true." And after a few more seconds, "What's *Mein Kampf*?"

"A book Hitler wrote. Not worth reading."

Red nodded.

"I see. Have you read it?"

"Glanced at it once. It's gibberish."

Art could see that Red looked agitated, but he didn't want to fan the flames. He was a little curious about the stranger. It was a good enough question: why would someone be interested in Brant Russell after all these years?

"Can I at least try to find out who he is, Chief?"

"Hitler?" Art said, grinning.

"Another zinger, Chief. No, the stranger at the library."

Art decided some exercise might be good for Red.

"Okay, Red. But quietly. See what you come up with. But remember, he might only be some guy killing time and reading old newspaper issues. Some people like to read crime stories. Don't assume he's Charlie Manson—you do know who Charlie Manson is, right?"

"I do. And I'll be discreet, Chief. Promise."

Art wondered whether Red truly appreciated what the word implied. But he had to admit that knowing more about the stranger might be prudent. Always know who's in your town, he reminded himself.

"That's fine—be discreet." Art looked up at the sky, at the darkening clouds. "Looks like some more of your ions are about to splash down."

Twelve

The Argus City Council convened on a Thursday night, as was its custom. Ralph Brooks, who owned the local Chevrolet dealership, chaired the council. He gaveled the group to order precisely at 7 p.m. and the five members waded through old business about street repairs, including a report from the city engineer. Art didn't bother to drop in until 7:30, when he knew they'd be closer to new business. Art's lack of uniform was the new business.

Art sat in the first row. As was *his* custom, he wore slacks and an oxford shirt and loafers. Only about a dozen folks had showed up, mostly people affected by the street repairs. After a while the mayor, Hedges Sullivan, came in and sat next to Art. Hedges, a silver-haired gentleman in his early sixties, was prone to ego and vanity and had a sharp eye for the ladies, but he did a good job of overseeing the town, Art knew. When Art had first been hired, he caught Sullivan banging his secretary, who definitely was not his wife, in his office, and ever since then Sullivan had resided comfortably in Art's hip pocket for future reference. The future had arrived.

Ralph Brooks announced it was time for new business, and Art and Hedges traded glances. Most of the people had left before new business. Art looked over his shoulder: there was one young man, someone he did not know. The man had a magazine and was looking down at it. Art took another look and realized he sort of fit the general description Red had of the so-called mysterious stranger, though this young man was clean-shaven. There were new people in town all the time and Art didn't give it another thought.

Ralph Brooks cleared his throat.

"Chief, thanks for coming by tonight."

"Glad to, Mr. Chairman."

"And the council recognizes that the mayor is in attendance, too," Ralph said.

"At your service, Ralph," Hedges said.

Ralph leaned back in his chair a moment as though he had suddenly forgotten how he wished to begin. Leaning forward, Ralph finally said, "The council has had the notion of looking into why Chief Millage no longer wears his uniform. And it's come to our attention the Chief also does not wear his weapon. Those are the items slotted under new business."

Ralph was beholden to Hedges, Art knew, because of some issues regarding overcharging the city for vehicle repairs that managed to get swept under the carpet. Three of the other council members were nice enough to Art and all guilty of varying degrees of malfeasance they would much prefer did not see the light of day. The wild card on the council was Caitlynn Rutherford. She was new to the council and an executive at State Farm in Bloomington, but she lived in a new and tony subdivision on Lake Argus. Her constituents were new money, new to town, and ambitious. And Republican, Art figured. They made their money in Bloomington and spent a lot of it there, too.

"I suppose the best way to start," Ralph said, "is to just ask Chief Millage if he would be so kind as to walk us through the— how he arrived at the decision to, uh—not to wear his uniform and weapon. Chief Millage?"

"Do you need me to stand?" Art said.

"Seated is just fine, Chief. We can hear you just fine."

"I appreciate that, Mr. Chairman."

Art crossed a leg over the other. His arms were crossed over his chest. He briefly wondered how they would perceive his body language. He didn't think he was consciously trying to send any messages. Maybe he was.

"Well, Ralph—and esteemed council members—I guess I'd start by reminding the council that I've been the police chief of Argus for fifteen years."

Ralph nodded vigorously, as though cued to do so.

"The council is very aware of your long service, Chief, dating back to 1970," Ralph said. "The council—the whole town—appreciates it, too."

Hedges half-rose from his chair.

"Ralph, can I just interject something here?"

Art didn't think Ralph looked particularly surprised by the mayor's sudden intrusion.

"Go ahead. By all means."

Hedges eased back into his chair. He wore a light blue silk shirt and red silk tie, and he was indeed someone with a commanding and handsome appearance. He had been mayor for twenty years. He had sold life insurance very successfully before that.

"Mr. Chairman, I just want to add that in addition to Art's long record of very exemplary service, there was a dark time in Argus history, during Art's very first year on the job, when a madman with a gun was on the loose, and that madman shot one of our esteemed sons just back from Vietnam, where he had served honorably and with distinction and valor, and thanks to Art, that madman was stopped and Argus was protected—preserved, I might say."

Art winced a little when Hedges started tossing out madman so liberally. Brant Russell had been many things, but madman wasn't likely one of them. He was just—unfortunate, really, with the choices he had made. But Art had to admit that Hedges could always deliver a fine speech. You'd think Dominick Cruikshank had been Audie Murphy to hear Hedges describe it.

"Duly noted, Mr. Mayor," Ralph said. "Duly noted. I do indeed remember that dark day very well. I have long said that Chief Millage stepped up into the breach that day and stood tall for this town. He was our general that day."

Art winced again. What a lot of gas, he thought. The breach? A general? For God's sake. Had it been the Charge of the Light Brigade for Christ's sake? Or Pickett's Charge at Gettysburg? Art also noticed that Caitlynn shifted uneasily in her chair. She had not lived in Argus in 1970. He wondered if she even knew the story.

"Mr. Chairman," she said. "I am unfamiliar with this dark day being mentioned here—so grandly, I might add. Could someone, uh, educate me as to what transpired?"

"May I have the honor of that task?" Hedges said quickly and Ralph gestured approval just as quickly.

It was all starting to resemble the courtroom scene from *To Kill a Mockingbird*, Art thought. He glanced over his shoulder at the young stranger, but the man seemed to still be reading his magazine.

Hedges unraveled the tale of Brant Russell, and Art endured it by trying very hard to think of casting his spinning rod on Lake Argus until Hedges had finished and Caitlynn seemed satisfied.

"Thank you, Mayor, for that inspiring and colorful story," she said. "Perhaps you should be a novelist."

Art sensed the subtle venom in the remark, but he felt that it sailed over Hedges' head by a country mile.

"Why, you're very welcome, young lady," Hedges said.

One of the other council members, Ted Sanders, who sold real estate, said, "Yes, yes, that was a very thorough story, but I think we were at the point of asking Chief Millage why he no longer wears a uniform and gun."

"Quite right, Ted," Caitlynn said energetically. The two exchanged smiles that Art felt were a tad nervous. He vaguely wondered whether the two of them were sleeping together. He made a mental note to ask Hedges about that. If anyone would know, it would be the mayor.

"That's correct," Ralph said. "Chief, you were saying?"

Art thought a moment, felt their eyes all over him. It had never quite come together until now, this evening with a spotlight trained his direction: but he believed he had simply earned the right to wear or not wear the uniform. It really was no more complicated than that. He had earned the right to not wear his gun. He had earned those damn rights because on one damn day he had put his own damn life on the line when Brant Russell had shot at him and he had done what nobody on that silly, preening council likely would have had the balls to do—take a life to protect lives. Their damn lives.

He told them that and watched eyes widen and several jaws drop a little, especially Caitlynn's. He did not think she was used to being lectured to at all. Well, Republicans have a lot coming to them. He paused to let it all sink in and soak them thoroughly before continuing.

"I have given myself to this town long enough for people to know who the Chief is," Art said. "And I don't need a uniform for that. I don't need a weapon for that. I have deputies well-armed and well-trained and they can be counted on, too. If that displeases the council, it can vote to make me put the uniform back on. Or perhaps one of you would care to wear the uniform and face the music when it's time to protect this town."

Art had stood, and he stared at them defiantly a moment before sitting. His palms were sweaty and his pulse had quickened. He felt sweat on his forehead. Hedges reached over and squeezed his elbow reassuringly. Ralph had sagged back into his chair. He asked whether anyone had further questions, but there were none. Caitlynn appeared to Art to have swallowed something distasteful the size of an anvil. She glanced at Ted, but he looked away into the distance. The other council members stole glances at Ralph, who Art thought seemed relieved.

The vote was four to one, with Caitlynn the lone voice desiring Art to wear his uniform and gun. That did not surprise him a bit. He now knew where he stood with her. He would watch his back with that one. Rumor had it that she wanted to run for mayor in a few years.

As he left the city building Hedges winked at him and went his own way. A couple of people who had stayed for the whole show patted Art on the back and said it was the right decision—

he'd earned it. They insisted he'd put in his time and had done his duty and had no reason to answer to anyone about the uniform and gun. Art thanked them and looked around for the young man who had been reading a magazine, but he was nowhere to be seen.

Thirteen

The rain had eased up, but folks around Argus still declared it one of the cooler summers they could remember in quite a spell. Even the fishing was slow to bounce back. Old Pete Armstrong, who ran the marina on Lake Argus, told Art the catfish were biting a little better, but the largemouth showed less interest and were quite stubborn. Art had swung by the marina to gas up his boat. He had taken the morning off before heading into town to check in at the station. His hours were his hours. As long as Hedges Sullivan was mayor and Ralph Brooks ran the council, Art ran his police force as he saw fit. He wondered if he would make twenty years as Chief. Twenty was always a milestone. And he'd done ten in Chicago. Thirty years as a cop. That would be something.

On the way to town, Art sensed he was being followed. It was subtle enough. A light blue Chevy Impala was a speck in his rearview mirror, but it had been there a while. He couldn't think of anyone who drove an Impala. He altered his route to town and the Impala stuck with him, though discreetly far back. Impulsively, he changed course again and drove out to Maggie Thomas's house. It had been a while since he had checked on her. And he wanted to get a better look at the Impala, which was still there.

Art pulled up Maggie's lane and got out quickly, before the Impala was in view. He slipped behind a thick tree trunk and when the car appeared, it slowed to a crawl at the mouth of the lane before continuing. Art got the plate number—it was a rental—but the window was up and the driver wore a baseball cap and sunglasses. He was male, but that was all Art could tell. He was uncertain about the age. He wrote down the plate number and waited a couple minutes to see if the car returned, but it didn't. He wasn't prepared to jump to any conclusions. It was a rental, so the driver could simply be lost. But he would check it out. Always know who people are, even if they're just lost.

He walked up to Maggie's porch, and she came out the door to greet him.

"My word, Chief. If anyone else was lurking behind one of my trees I might swat them with a broom."

Art laughed. He could imagine her as a teacher, threatening any student who had dared to lock swords with her.

"I believe you would."

"You *know* I would, Chief. I sat there in the window a while, watching. But I knew you must be doing something worth doing."

"Call me Art. The Chief is another fella." He reached the porch and sat in the swing. Maggie sat in a lawn chair.

"What *were* you doing, Art?"

He glanced down the lane toward the road, half-expecting to see the Impala roll by. *Stop that,* he told himself, *before you turn into Red and get too excited over someone lost out in the country.*

"I don't know. I guess I had a funny feeling someone was tailing me. But maybe not. I stopped for a better look."

"Did you figure it out?"

He shook his head.

"Couldn't see enough of the driver. And I didn't know the car. It was a rental, though, and easy enough to check."

"Probably lost, Chief. I've had folks pull up the lane and ask me how to get back out to the interstate. Or over to Bloomington."

"Probably nothing," Art said.

"Art, how about a beer?"

"Yeah, I'd drink one with you. I just had some lunch, so I can afford a beer. But just one."

"A Chief rule," she said.

"Got to have *some* rules."

She retrieved two very cold PBRs.

"You must have been working outside this morning," Art said after his first sip. It was very cold.

She grinned.

"How'd you figure that?"

"You once told me you reward yourself with a cold beer after working at something around your place."

"You should be a cop, Art."

"Maybe I'll give it a try some time."

"Don't rush into anything," she said. "I was out picking up all the branches after that big wind we had come up the other night. It rattled the windows, and I even worried it might be a tornado."

He nodded.

"I had the same problem out at the lake. That night the whitecaps on the lake looked big enough to surf on."

"A tornado would have us picking up our butts all over tarnation," she said.

"I've never actually seen one. Not in fifteen years in Argus."

"They've been around," she said. "But the good Lord had them land elsewhere, I guess. When I was a girl, I saw one a few miles north of here. It touched down and flattened a barn and drove sections of wood through trees. But then it just up and disappeared as quick as it came."

"How old were you?"

"I reckon I was ten. That would make it about 1915. The war had just gotten going over in Europe."

He was amazed at how much of her life she had lived, and how much she had seen and endured before he was even born.

"How you doing these days?" he said.

"Doing good. Knock wood." She reached over and knocked on the wood porch railing.

"Any visitors lately?"

"You mean Lucy Jean?"

She looked sad for a moment but composed herself.

"Yes, Lucy Jean."

She shook her head and sipped her beer.

"No, she hasn't paid a call lately. I suspect she's busy where she's at. And I've had housework and yard work. As we get older, Art, we do sometimes get better at having family living elsewhere."

"I guess that's so."

He wondered briefly about her use of the word living.

"What about your family, Art? Your parents, I mean. They still with us?"

"Yes, they are. Retired down in Clearwater, Florida. They've visited up here a few times over the years. We stay in touch by phone."

"They have good health?"

"Last I heard. They're both in their early seventies but do okay. We expect them up here later in the year. We drove down there last year."

"That's good, Art. You're blessed."

He nodded.

"Sometimes I think that's true."

"It *is* true. The hard part is recognizing it and then accepting it."

He thought, *Red really does underestimate this woman. He finished his beer and stood up.*

"Well, I have to get to town."

"Chief business?" she said.

"That's right. Time to put on my cape and tights. Thanks for the beer."

He stepped off the porch and turned and waved to her.

"Cold beer served here, Art. Anytime."

"Duly noted, Maggie."

He got into his car and backed down the lane onto the county road and was nearly to Argus before he remembered to run the plates on that light blue Impala.

Fourteen

Art had Red run the Impala plates.

"His name is Nathan Bedford. Seymour, Indiana. He's twenty-three, no record."

Art sipped his coffee and looked out his office window. Seymour, Indiana, he thought. Just like Brant Russell. So, he *was* being followed. He was glad to know his cop instincts were still intact. But things had suddenly become complicated.

Red looked a little confused.

"Say, Chief, isn't Seymour, Indiana, where Brant Russell was from, too?"

"That's right."

"That's some coincidence."

Art looked at Red and smirked.

"There are no coincidences."

Red nodded and then smiled.

"Oh. Yeah, I see. He probably knew Brant Russell—since they're from the same town."

"But he would have only been about eight years old."

Art had quickly done the math, which made the curious presence of Nathan Bedford even more interesting.

"Who, Chief?"

"Red, do you need another cup of your famous coffee before you wake up?"

Red blushed a little.

"Sorry. You mean that this Bedford was eight when Russell died."

"Bingo. Which begs the question, what was Russell to Bedford? Not brothers, but perhaps half-brothers? Cousins? What we do know is he's here, and he does seem connected to Russell after all."

"And he followed you, Chief."

"That was his first mistake. If he cared to remain anonymous, that is. Now we know he's no tourist, no fisherman, and not lost."

Red shifted weight from foot to foot.

"Should I haul him in?"

Art nearly choked on his coffee.

"For what? Jesus. It's not illegal to follow a cop. It's just not polite. Do we arrest him for bad manners?"

Red tried to say something, but nothing came out.

"And, Red, we really don't know that Bedford is the same guy who showed up at the library, now do we?"

"No, Chief. We don't. But doesn't it seem likely?"

"Yes. I grant you that one. But we need to be sure. That's your first job."

Red's face brightened.

"There is at least one *potential* coincidence, though," Art said.

"What's that, Chief?"

"The man's name—Nathan Bedford. Pretty damn close to Nathan Bedford Forrest."

"Who?"

Art smiled. History surely was a lost art among people Red's age. Art had always enjoyed it, especially when it concerned the Civil War.

"Nathan Bedford Forrest. Didn't they teach history when you were in school? He was a Confederate cavalry general, in the Civil War. The North feared him as much as they respected Lee."

"Sorry. Never heard of him."

"But you have heard of *Lee*, though—right?"

"Robert E. Lee," Red said emphatically. "Yes, sir. Everybody knows that one."

Art sniffed and studied Red's face a moment.

"You do know which *side* Lee fought on, right?"

"I think so—the wrong side, Chief?"

"Good answer. But you should read more."

"I am, Chief. Remember the other day? Ionization?"

"I stand corrected," Art said. "But you should also know who Forrest was. He started the Ku Klux Klan after the war, for example. They say the war likely never really ended for Forrest until he died."

Red nodded gravely.

"That's some coincidence, Chief—this guy having a name so close to Forrest."

"Maybe not. Maybe not at all. Indiana was once a hotbed for the Klan."

"Really? I always thought all that was down south somewhere. You know, like Alabama and Mississippi."

"Stupidity and hate are never confined to just one place."

Art sipped his coffee and looked again out the window, at the grove of trees.

After a moment, Red said, "So, what do we do now, Chief?"

"We need to eventually meet our Mr. Nathan Bedford."

"How?"

"That shouldn't be too hard, really. He sure seems to know how to find me. We'll let him do the heavy lifting on that one. Leave that to me."

"What do I do, Chief?"

"Get a hold of someone in Indiana. He has a driver's license, it would seem. Let's see if we can get a picture of Mr. Bedford."

"Right. I'm on it."

Art wasn't sure whether to be pleased or worried, and he stopped Red as he left the office.

"Go easy, Red. Go slowly. There's no crime here that we know of. He has no record. Keep that in mind."

"Okay, Chief." Red left, and Art could hear him skipping down the hall.

Art sipped coffee and stared out at the trees. What did Nathan Bedford want? And who was he to Brant Russell? Art was pondering it deeply when a thought occurred to him: what if Bedford wasn't Russell's half-brother or cousin at all? He recalled that Russell had no family—no brothers or sisters of record, his parents dead.

What if Bedford was Russell's son?

Suddenly, Art felt sick to his stomach.

Fifteen

Red got Bedford's photo from Indiana, and Art had it with him the next day as he drove to Bloomington. He had taken Doc Finch's advice after all, and there was a sudden opening with Dr. Holden, a psychiatrist. He parked at the doctor's office and studied the photo: Nathan Bedford struck Art as rather birdlike with a pointed nose and a slim face—lightly bearded in the photo. He had brown hair, perhaps medium length—almost shaggy, really. The boy was not ugly, but Art did not think he qualified as handsome, either. The face could hide well in a crowd. He checked the vitals: five-ten and one-ninety. Stout. The size of a cornerback in the NFL. He absently wondered if the boy had played football. Art had played safety in high school.

In the waiting room, Art picked through magazines until he found a Sports Illustrated. He did not really feel like reading but glanced at pictures of football players. The Bears were in training camp up in Wisconsin and Art did read a short article about their prospects for 1985.

The receptionist showed him into Dr. Holden's office. The doctor was shelving a book in a massive bookcase. The wood looked quite old to Art. The office itself seemed antiseptic clean and Art even thought it faintly smelled like some cleaner had been used recently. The chairs and desk also struck Art as very old. Antiques, perhaps. They contrasted sharply with the doctor, who was perhaps forty but dressed younger, had sideburns at a fashionable length, and wore tinted glasses that seemed a bit Hollywoodish for Bloomington, Illinois.

"May I call you Art?" Dr. Holden said, offering a hand and a smile a dentist would love.

Art shook hands with him. The man had a decent grip and Art appreciated that it wasn't wimpy.

"Art's fine, doctor."

"Walt—if that's okay with you. All that doctor business can get in the way sometimes."

Art thought that all that doctor business might actually be why folks showed up here at all, but he let it go. Walt gestured for Art to sit in a padded, high-back chair and then he slipped into his own chair behind the desk.

"Thanks, Walt." Art got comfortable in the seat, though he vaguely felt like a high school kid in the principal's office. "And thanks for getting me in on short notice."

"My pleasure," Walt said. "Thad Finch is an old family friend. I'm always glad to be of service to his patients."

Art had a hard time seeing himself as a patient. But no one had twisted his arm to make the visit.

"So, Art, what brings you here today?"

Art decided he might just expedite things by being direct.

"I've killed people, Walt."

"How many?" Walt said.

Art thought Walt had said it as though he could be asking how many eggs Art had had for breakfast. Art figured the man likely had heard some amazing stuff while holding the hands of strangers.

"Two, Walt."

"I see. In the line of duty, I presume."

"No, just randomly," Art said, curious to see how far humor would go and regretting it immediately, though the only reaction he got from Walt was a very thin smile.

"But they happened many years ago, didn't they?" Walt said.

"How'd you know?" Art wondered whether he had read up on him somehow.

"If they were fresh, you might not be joking about them so easily."

Art nodded, felt appropriately scolded.

"I can see how that might be true."

A moment of silence settled between them. Art noticed that Walt was good at maintaining the thin smile and keeping eye contact without seeming too intimidating.

"You don't wear a uniform, Art. Or a gun. Or is that just for this visit?"

"No, this is me now, day to day."

"I see."

Art was already tired of that phrase.

"How long since you ditched the uniform and gun?"

Ditched, Art thought. *Was he trying to sound hip, cool? It made it sound like he had tossed them from a speeding car.*

"Recently. At the start of summer."

"I see. How long did you wear the uniform—and gun?"

"Fifteen years. And ten before that, in Chicago."

Walt drummed his fingers lightly on his desk a moment, and then leaned forward in his chair.

"Art, let me ask you this—what did you hope to get from coming here today?"

Art blinked a couple times and shifted in his chair.

"I don't know."

"Can you tell me why you no longer wear the uniform and gun?"

Art remembered the night he addressed the city council. He'd been pretty clear and direct about it then. But how true had it all been?

"I was asked that question by the city council. Just the other day."

"What did you tell them?"

"That it was none of their business, really."

"They bought that?"

"By a four to one vote, yes they did."

"Good for you, Art. Congratulations, my friend."

Art saw just how subtle the sarcasm was. The man was good.

"You're not really congratulating me," Art said.

Walt shrugged.

"Does it matter? You got what you wanted, right?"

Art had been around long enough to know when he was being baited.

"There's more to it than—than just winning the argument."

"So tell me about that."

Art shifted in the chair, even though it was very comfortable. The high back made him feel a little too enclosed, like he was in the grasp of something. His palms were moist.

"I no longer feel comfortable in the uniform."

Art knew that to be true. But he couldn't have told the council that.

Walt appeared to weigh Art's statement.

"But you're the Chief of Police. Chiefs wear uniforms and badges and carry guns."

"Most do. That's not in dispute here."

"What is in dispute?"

Walt had raised his voice a little, but Art managed not to react to it.

"Identity?" Art finally said.

"Good. Tell me about identity. Who are you, Art?"

And then Art knew. He was amazed at how easily it just came to him. It seeped up from very deep and stared him in the face with great and thunderous clarity: he wanted a new identity, needed a new identity. It was true. But he didn't know what it was, what it could be. That unknown scared him. For the first time since that day in early spring, he began to cry again, softly. He wiped the tears away with the back of a hand.

"Sorry—I'm sorry."

"That's okay." Walt pushed a box of tissues across the desk and Art used one to dab his eyes.

"Crying is a release, Art. We need it. You need it. Go ahead. Let things go."

Art managed to compose himself. He did feel oddly better.

"That usually doesn't happen," Art said.

"But it *has* happened before, hasn't it?"

Art thought back to spring, back to falling in the mud and crying and having no idea why.

"Yes, it has."

"It's good to cry," Walt said. "It can be cleansing."

"I get that," Art said.

"No, you probably don't. But you will later."

Later, Art thought. *How much later? Tomorrow? Next week?*

"So, Walt, what do I do now?"

"What do you *want* to do?"

"I don't know." Art's eyes were still very moist, and he dabbed at them again. "I can tell you this much—I can't kill again. I can't do that again. Not ever."

Walt nodded.

"I thought we might end up there, Art."

Sixteen

Art had invited a very surprised Red out to the lake to go fishing on Saturday. Art knew that Red had grown up on the lake, and so he let him pilot the boat down to the bay south of Stevenson Point. Red wisely set the throttle at half and steered into clouds of mist cautiously and stood for a better view of what was ahead.

Art was happy to relax in the passenger seat. The visit with Dr. Holden was still on his mind a little, but he was working past it. He wasn't even sure he would go back. He felt he'd said his piece. His dilemmas were out in the open. It had been a little painful, but useful. He figured it was up to him now to deal with them and not some doctor.

Once inside the mouth of the bay, Red chopped the throttle, and they floated toward shore slowly and in casting range of reeds and submerged tree trunks. Art thought it was marvelously quiet, just the sound of waves lapping shore. Old Pete Armstrong at the marina had assured them that the fish seemed to be hungry again, though the largemouth could still be a little balky. Art had brought a cooler, along with a six-pack of Pabst and some roast beef sandwiches that Carolyn had volunteered to make for them the night before.

They both retrieved fishing rods from gunwales and attached reels in silence. It was very early morning, and mist persisted on the lake's surface. When they were done, they paused to finish their coffee. Well outside the mouth of the bay, a lone outboard could be heard but not seen because of the mist.

"These foggy mornings are dangerous," Red said. "When I was a little kid out here, two boats collided. One of the drivers was killed. The other was fished out half-drowned."

Art nodded.

"I think I recall hearing about that. Just before I got to town, I think."

"Sixty-eight or nine," Red said. "I was just learning how to water-ski."

"Were they locals or summer people, Red?"

"Summer people."

"Figures. How old were you back then?"

"Nine, I reckon. Maybe ten."

Art could imagine that even then Red was probably a fiery red-headed boy given to being impetuous, but likeable. A scamp was what it was called in his day.

"While you were waterskiing, I took over as Chief."

"You've been Chief quite a while, Chief."

"Yes, I sure have." Art reflected on whether it was the length of time or the mileage that inevitably eroded a man. He added, "Out here, it might make sense if you called me Art. Back in town, we can always play the power and authority game."

"Is that how you really see it—Art."

"Yeah, pretty much."

Red strung his line from the open-face reel up through the eyelets.

"By the way, Chief, there's nothing new on Nathan Bedford. No one has seen him since that last day he tailed you."

Art glanced at Red and nodded, then hefted his spinning rod in one hand and assessed how it felt. It was a very light Fenwick with a graphite shaft and had cost more than he had ever thought he would spend for a rod.

"Art, Red. Just call me Art out here. We're fishing."

"I know," Red said. "But this was Chief business, so I called you Chief for Chief business."

Art nodded.

"That's fine. Makes sense. Anything else you want to say about Bedford? He's not fishing with us today."

Red laid his spinning rod across his lap.

"Well, maybe he's gone. Maybe he's just gone on home, back to Seymour Fucking Indiana, where he belongs."

Art fiddled with the bale on his reel.

"Maybe."

Art tied a Rapala to his line and Red tried a Lazy Ike. Both were good and proven lures. Now that they were ready to begin casting, Art knew that an unwritten ritual of fishing would settle in: men would cast in silence, focused on the mechanics of casting and placing the lures as close to targets as possible until someone caught a fish or at least had a strike. Then it would be okay to chat as they fished. Those first casts, with the lake still waking up, would be a time of tension and expectation. Art enjoyed it and cherished it as time away from the world. He didn't have to be the Chief out on the lake.

After his fifth cast, Art glanced at the mouth of the bay: the mist was finally clearing away and he could see a good portion of the main channel of the lake. The water was calm and bluish-green. His sixth cast landed near a tree stump and produced a solid strike. He pulled back hard and set the hook and reeled a bit but yielded some line to the fish when it made a dash back toward the stump. He was able to regain some line, and the fish broached the surface once with a sharp splash, and Art saw it was a largemouth bass. Then he felt the line slacken and knew the fish had slipped the lure.

"Easy come, easy go," Art said to Red, but Art had enjoyed the fight and was grinning.

"I think he had some size to him," Red said.

"Felt like he did," Art said. "He sure felt like he did."

Art felt the adrenaline.

Soon Red had caught several good-sized crappies, and then Art caught one, too. By eleven, their arms were tired, and they had enough crappie on ice to fuel a decent fish fry.

Art put his rod down.

"Well, I think it's safe to drink a beer. It's noon *somewhere*.

"In Mogadishu, Art. It's noon in Mogadishu."

"Actually, I think it might be *tomorrow* in Mogadishu, but close enough."

"Where is Mogadishu?" Red said.

Art had to really think.

"Somalia? I think so."

"It's a funny name, Mogadishu," Red said. "I remember it from a high school history class for some reason. Funny what comes to you when you're out fishing. Funny what you remember from school. It's like you're able to think beyond your daily life out here."

"I think that's likely so," Art said. He fished two PBRs out of the cooler and handed one to Red.

"Thanks, Chief. Art, I mean."

"Salute," Art said, and they both took hearty swigs.

"That's cold beer," Red said. "But awfully good."

Art raised his can in salute.

"To cold beer and warm women."

"I can drink to that, Art."

"You better. I'd have to take your badge if you couldn't."

They clinked their cans together.

"You wouldn't want it the other way around," Red said. "Warm beer and cold women."

"Damn good point there, Red. You'll go far in life."

At wondered what Red would be like drunk.

"Red, do you have a girlfriend?"

It had occurred to Art that he knew very little about Red, even though he had been his deputy for five years.

"I do. You know her—Mary Peterson. She works at the bank."

"One of the tellers?"

"Uh-huh. Long dark hair and a championship chest."

Red opened his hands over his chest for emphasis.

"Got it," Art said. "I know which one she is, sure."

"She's hard to miss."

Art decided to sidestep that one.

"The two of you serious?"

"Maybe. It's been two years now. You think I should get married?"

"Do you *want* to get married?"

"We talked about it once," Red said. "I don't know."

"Maybe that's your answer," Art said. "If you aren't sure, maybe you shouldn't. At least for now. You have to be able to tell yourself you really love her and really want to stay together. Marriage is hard work and full of compromises."

Red sat his empty can down.

"We fight sometimes, and over little things. Pissant things."

"Part of the deal, Red. But if you marry the right one, the good days outnumber the bad ones, and you work your way through the little skirmishes back to the good days."

"I hope so," Red said. "You waited some years to get married."

Art looked out the mouth of the bay to the main channel. It was very clear, and the water was still. A sailboat with a blue sail traversed the far shore, and it was very small at that distance.

"I guess I waited until I found someone as good as Carolyn. And I married up, as they say. Another beer, Red?"

"Is the pope Catholic?"

Art grinned and handed Red a beer.

"Well, if he isn't, he's missed a hell of an opportunity."

Seventeen

Art had heard that Old Pete Armstrong was of a mind to sell the Lake Argus marina. At first, Art didn't think much about it at all. The story went that Old Pete and his wife had a little condo in Florida and were ready to go sit and watch the sun set on a bigger body of water. But after the weekend and fishing with Red, Art had thought about it more and drove out there.

Old Pete was tightening a clamp on one of the pump hoses. Art knew that he was called Old Pete because his face was permanently tanned and weathered like old leather after a lifetime on Lake Argus. But Pete was only sixty-two. That didn't seem old to Art.

Pete looked up as Art strolled onto the marina deck.

"Looking for some desperado, Chief?"

"I have deputies who wish that were true. How are you?"

"Pretty fair, Chief. Pretty fair."

"Call me Art, if you will."

"Okay, Art. I did hear you don't go by Chief much anymore. And you don't wear the uniform. How's that working out?"

"Working out just fine for me," Art said.

"Maybe not so well for some folks on the council, though."

"Good news travels fast, I guess."

"And Caitlin Rutherford gasses her boat here, Art. She's a got a big mouth."

"Careful," Art said. "She's likely the next mayor, in about two years."

"You think so?"

"Could be. She's been running unofficially ever since she got on the council. She's got ambition. And Hedges won't run again. He's had enough."

"How would all that sit with you?"

"That's a bridge way down the road," Art said. "Not my concern right now."

Pete wiped his hands with a rag.

"And what *is* your concern? If you don't mind my asking."

"I don't mind a bit. I heard you want to sell and move on."

"It's time," Pete said. "I've been fortunate and made a couple bucks and can afford to move on now. This is my last season."

"How long have you been out here?"

"Almost thirty-six years. I bought the place from my uncle."

"You must have started off pretty young, Pete."

"I was maybe twenty-six. But I had worked construction since high school and saved money to make a decent down payment on the place. I even put off getting hitched until I had this place bought."

Art nodded and walked to the end of the deck and took stock of the place: three gas pumps and a small store that sold most things people on the lake needed during summer. Next door was The Night Owl diner, which paid Pete rent to sit on the property. Both businesses fed each other very well. The marina closed from November to March, but Art had heard it always did well enough to take the time off. Pete employed a couple kids each season to pump gas and man the register and stopped by every day to keep things straight. A gas station was a gas station, whether on land or water, and gas stations made good money. Art was beginning to wonder if he could buy the place and make a go of it. He had worked for others all his life and figured it was time to work for himself. He was not really all that surprised he'd reached the conclusion.

He walked back over to Pete, who was putting tools back in his toolbox.

"Any offers, Pete?"

"Haven't listed it just yet. I talk to a realtor this week, though."

"Would you sell it to me?"

Pete stared at Art a few seconds.

"You serious?"

"I might be. Yeah."

Pete took off his Cardinals baseball cap and ran a hand through his bristly hair.

"Marinas cost more than most folks might think," Pete said. "I just thought I'd toss that out there for you in case you had the notion it's like buying a second car or such."

Art appreciated Pete's directness.

"I've been a cop for twenty-five years and took care of my money. My house is paid for and I've got a couple retirement plans to fall back on, too. I can put down a good amount if you were to do that kind of deal with me—like the deal that got you started."

Pete nodded, but Art could see he was still skeptical.

"Have you talked this through with your wife—with Carolyn?"

"No, and I have to, for sure. That's next. I just got the idea. But I am serious."

"Art, you do know what sort of money we're talking about here, don't you?"

"More than what they get for a second car."

Pete grinned.

"I *would* prefer to sell to someone with character *and* a sense of humor."

Art smiled.

"How much, Pete?"

"A sliver or two under two-hundred grand. Still interested?

"That's some coin, I admit."

"Well, it'd be the bank's money," Pete said. "Gas revenues would service the debt and give you a nice amount each month clear and above. Diner rent in the offseason pays against your loan payment, too. A damn solid investment."

Art did some hasty math in his head. "I suspect I could put down as much as twenty-five percent," Art said.

"And that's just that much less you'd owe the bank," Pete said.

Art wondered how Carolyn would react. He didn't even have a notion how it might go. He would have to make the case that it was good for both of them. But if it panned out, it could be his ticket out of being a cop, finally. A new identity, for sure.

"Let me run it by Carolyn tonight. We've always had an equal say in everything we do. I need her on board to do it. Would you give me a day to get back to you?"

Pete nodded.

"Sure, Art. I will. That realtor isn't coming out from Bloomington for a couple days."

"And can we keep this between us for now?"

"No reason for me to mention it to anyone, Art. None at all."

Art offered a hand and they shook.

"I'll come by tomorrow," Art said. "Thanks, Pete." He walked off the deck onto land.

"Art," Pete called. "Art, do you think you would *like* running a marina?"

Art placed his hands on his hips and looked out over the sparkling water and felt the warm sun scrub his face. Whenever he was at Lake Argus he felt—free.

"Yeah. I believe I would."

Eighteen

Art took the long way home and drove a circuit around the lake to have time to think about the marina and what he might be getting into. He was excited. But would Carolyn go for the idea? He could think of no reason she wouldn't, though he had to admit he wasn't sure, off the top of his head, why she would, either.

But they had a solid marriage and talked to each other. There were no long brooding silences. When things came up, invariably they got dumped on the kitchen table over coffee or a scotch and hashed out between the two of them. Coffee for the low-level stuff and scotch for when things were more complicated. Sometimes they ended up a little drunk, but always they addressed the issues.

Could he really buy the marina? Yes. Of course. Money wasn't the issue. Over the years Art had accumulated certificates of deposit. There was more than enough there to do twenty-five percent down. The bank would do the loan, he was sure. Their house was paid for and good collateral. It was worth more than $100,000 and the value would keep climbing on any house on the lake with a good view of a bay. And he was the Chief, still. The bank would respect and honor that.

What else? He had those retirement plans for the day he needed them. Carolyn made good money teaching and planned to teach another ten years. She had paid into her own retirement plan for more than twenty-five years. The marina would provide a nice income those ten years and then, like Old Pete, Art could choose to sell out, too, and pocket the equity. The marina would also keep Art on the lake and out of the line of fire. Literally and figuratively.

He had hoped to last twenty years as Chief, but it no longer mattered. He was finally resolved to that. At most, he could gut out two more years, until Caitlin Rutherford likely became mayor, and then his days would be numbered. She would eventually get the council to demand he put the uniform and gun back on, and Art would never do that. He could afford not to. He would quit first.

But he did have fifteen-plus years on the job and he was proud of his record. He had taken care of Argus. No one could ever dispute that or take it away. He had put his life on the line with Brant Russell and protected the town that day. Twenty would have been nice, something to look back on, the old traditional milestone, but fifteen was good enough now. It seemed better every day. Toss in his ten years in Chicago and Art could lay claim to an even bigger milestone—twenty five. It truly and really was something, and he felt a great sense of accomplishment and satisfaction wash over him, despite what the price of carrying a gun had been.

Art supposed he would have to stay on the job into fall because it appeared Pete would finish the season before hanging it up. That was fine. No problem. He had decisions that would need to be made—serious decisions, such as, who would the next Chief be? He wanted to be part of that process. He truly cared about Argus. And he had begun to wonder if Red could take over. At least in the interim, and maybe he could demonstrate with that opportunity that he should keep the job.

Red had been his Chief Deputy five years and had grown a little each year. Art could sense that despite his impetuous nature, Red was learning the lessons about patience and logic and being rational in making decisions. Art had been a bit impetuous at that age, too, but he knew Red was likely already growing out of it. To be Chief, he would have to. He felt sure, with the backing of Hedges Sullivan, that Ralph Brooks and the council would at least sign off on Red as interim Chief.

As he drove, he realized he would have a long period of time on his hands for the first time in twenty-five years. Pete would ride out the marina season until November before the big skedaddle to Florida and the marina would close until March. Over Christmas break, he could take Carolyn down to Florida, too, and visit his folks, instead of having them make that long drive up. What else would he do with the time? He didn't know but was excited by that unknown. He would discover things to do, and that process would be a new adventure for him. A new life. That new identity he had come to acknowledge with Dr. Holden. At spring break, maybe he could take Carolyn on another trip, somewhere they had never been, but had talked about, like New Orleans, or California. Maybe Arizona. Or Santa Fe, a town he had heard was beautiful and laid back. Art felt he might need a larger landscape to inhabit from time to time. But at his core, he knew he wanted more time on Lake Argus. It was home.

As he reached the dam, he abruptly turned off and drove down where he could see the spillway. With the recent rain, the lake level was up and there might be enough flow below the dam to produce foamy whitewater. Art had always enjoyed seeing that. It made him think of the wild trout streams and their rapids in places well north, like Michigan. And the sound of the flowing water was soothing.

He parked and walked over to the spillway edge. There was good flow after all, and the roar of the rushing water was loud enough to mask all other sounds once he was standing right next to it. He checked his watch. Still some time before Carolyn would get home from school. He thought some more about Red becoming Chief. That day of fishing had produced a more thoughtful side to Red, and Art was happy to see that. He had always liked the boy and had wanted to give him an opportunity, and now he could say he also knew him more as a person and that it validated his affection for him. He would ease off the teasing and the jokes and afford Red more respect. He had earned it.

Art stood a while and watched the rushing, foamy water. It could even be a little hypnotic, he conceded and could allow one to forget what was around and really focus on the things that mattered—or not think at all. It was good either way. Standing there, he could just be.

After a few minutes he turned away from the roaring water and walked up the gentle slope to his car, and as he reached level ground, he caught a flash of blue out of the corner of an eye. Looking up, at the road above the spillway, he saw the light blue Impala, and Nathan Bedford staring at him through an open window.

Nineteen

Art stood next to his car for a minute after Bedford had driven away. There was no reason to overreact. For what? Okay, so the guy was back in circulation. Big surprise. Art had never truly believed he was gone, just simmering somewhere. Why simmering? Well, because the kid must surely want something from him. And it clearly had to be connected to Brant Russell. Simmering likely was as good a word for it as any.

Who the fuck was Nathan Bedford?

One thing was certain: Bedford had gotten better at tailing people.

Art shook his head and winced. Clearly there might be one last battle of sorts to fight before he had earned his chance for peace. Good Lord. He hoped it wasn't a fight that was coming. Plenty of things could be worked out. Whatever this was, maybe it was negotiable. Most things were. It might only be curiosity on Bedford's part. But Art could still see the look on Bedford's face: it had been cold and hard.

Art worried that in his place Red might have jumped in his car and chased Bedford. Or maybe not. He had to remember to give Red more credit. The boy was learning. He was likely the Chief soon enough, too. It very well could be that how Bedford ultimately got handled could be a crucial audition for Red.

Art drove to town, watching his rearview mirror, but the blue Impala didn't appear again. At the station, Scotty Gaines was the only deputy there. He was at a desk looking over some papers. He was a good man but had been on the force just a year. He was still greener than green. And Art wanted calm to be the defining aspect of what was coming. Whatever it was.

"Scotty, when you get a second would you get on the horn and ask Red to amble on over here."

"Sure, Chief. Right away. Everything okay?"

Art forced a grin, squeezed Scotty's shoulder.

"Just fine. Do we have fresh coffee?"

"Red made some before he went out."

"My lucky day," Art said, noting the irony. He poured a cup of coffee in the ready room and then went to his office and closed the door.

When Red reached the station, Art was drinking a second cup of coffee and had rested his legs on the edge of his desk to look out the window at the grove of trees. And he had retrieved his revolver from a desk drawer. It sat on his desk in its holster.

"Pull up a chair, Red—and close the door, too."

When Red had sat down, Art said, "Bedford's back."

"I know, Chief."

"You know?" Art swung his legs off the desk to the floor. "When we're you going to tell me?"

"I just saw him a couple minutes ago, when I got to town, Chief. He was gassing up down at Gilstrap's."

Art nodded.

"Okay. Sorry about that."

"No problem, Chief."

"The door's closed. Call me Art."

"Does Scotty know any of this?"

"Not yet. He'll know if it becomes necessary for him to know."

"Makes sense. Where'd *you* see Bedford, Art?"

"Out by the dam spillway."

Red appeared to mull that a moment.

"What were you doing out there?"

"I like watching the overflow water." Art shrugged. "When I looked up, there he was, sitting on the road looking down at me."

"He's gotten better at tailing."

"I guess he has, Red. Or I'm getting too lax. A little of both, I reckon. But now we need to get better at finding out who the fuck he is, and why he's here. He doesn't get to be a tourist anymore, Red. I saw his face. He didn't look like a happy camper."

"What's our plan?"

"First off, we have to know who he really is to Brant Russell." Art winced and stared out the window at the trees. "I do have a theory."

"You think he still might be a cousin, or even a half-brother to Russell?" Red said.

"No." Art didn't look at Red. "I don't know that for sure, but that's not what my gut says."

"What, then?"

Art swiveled back toward Red.

"His son, maybe. How does that strike you?"

"Damn," Red said. "That would make a huge difference."

"I guess it would, Red."

"He'd be the right age and all."

"Now you're being analytical—good." Art eased back in his chair and sighed heavily. "It explains it better than cousin or even half-brother. Those things might conjure up curiosity. But being the son, well, that could take the equation a whole lot further down the road."

"Revenge?"

"You're learning, Red. That's exactly what it could be. Maybe he thinks it's his job to avenge the father he never really knew and all that shit. Who knows? But we have to find out."

Red shifted in his chair. "Maybe he's just curious. Maybe he just wanted to see where it happened. For perspective, I guess. I don't know."

Art frowned. "He didn't seem like a man looking for perspective. He looked like a man with a problem and unsure how to deal with it. That can be dangerous."

Red nodded.

"Now what?"

"Don't you want to just go arrest him, Red?"

"For what? For following a cop and having a shitty look on his face?" Red tacked a grin on at the end.

"Good answer, Red. Good answer." Art had needed to feel Red would be reliable and rational. "But now we need to know the whole story of Mr. Nathan Bedford."

Red looked down. "I should have checked more into him when I got his name and photo from Indiana. I screwed up."

"No, you didn't. There was no reason to at the time. He had no record, had committed no crimes. But now, yeah—find out who the bastard really is."

Red got up and opened the door and looked back.

"What are you going to do, Chief?"

Art looked out the window.

"I'm going to sit here and finish my coffee and wait for you to tell me what's out there waiting for us."

After Red had gone, Art stared for a while at the gun on his desk.

Art daydreamed for some time about how he would approach Carolyn about buying the marina. He believed he would convince her. With eyes closed he saw himself in a t-shirt and shorts, a man who had shed a public image as heavy as armor, cruising in his boat to his marina, beholden to no one except Carolyn.

Then Red came back and sat down.

"You're right, Art. He's the son all right."

The image of the marina was shut down as quickly as flipping a switch. *So, there it was,* Art thought. *It's out in the open now. Brant Russell had a son, and now he's come to call.* He had a fleeting thought of Brant Russell dead and himself standing over the body.

"Who'd you talk to?"

"The Chief over in Seymour. He claims Bedford never actually met his dad. His mother never told Russell about the boy."

"A story for the movies," Art said quietly. "What else?"

"Nothing that really stands out. No record, of course. Some horseplay fights in high school, but nothing major. He played football a couple years. He went to work as a machinist in some pissant widget factory over there after high school."

"Football," Art said. "I thought so. Did you play, Red?"

Red appeared surprised by the question.

"A little. My sophomore and junior years."

"I played safety," Art said. "How about you?"

"Receiver. But our quarterback couldn't really throw all that well."

"Were you any good, Red?"

"I could catch the ones he threw. There weren't all that many. How about you?"

"I did okay, too," Art said. "Football's a dandy game."

Red looked amused.

"Is this relevant, Art?"

"Not a bit. But we *could* just ask Bedford to come by and relive our gridiron glory days together."

"Funny, Chief."

"Humor's important in deals like this. Believe me."

"I believe you."

Art got up and went to the window. Through the trees he could still see a good stretch of Main Street and he looked around to see if Bedford's car was there, but he didn't really expect to see it parked right out front, Bedford leaning against a bumper with a smug look on his face. *But that would sure simplify things,* Art thought. If that were the case, he'd just pop out the front door and ask Mr. Nathan Bedford none too gently what his intentions were, and they'd know pretty damn quick which direction this thing was going.

He turned back to Red.

"What we've got here is a wild card. Now we know *why* he's here, but not what he intends to do—if anything. So far, he's been playing cat and mouse."

"Maybe that's his plan," Red said. "Maybe that's all he's got. Just, come over for a look and try to jerk you around some."

Art looked back out the window.

"There probably wasn't a plan. Not at first. He probably *did* just one day reach the conclusion to come over here and see where it happened."

"And the man who killed his father," Red said.

"That, too." But Art was surprised at how he felt. Instead of regret, he felt annoyed. Annoyed that this killing he could not have avoided was being dragged back out of history for no good reason. This boy out there, Bedford, couldn't change a damn thing and wallowing in it could cause only harm. *Let it go*, Art thought. *Let it go before it consumes you—and me.*

Red stood up and joined Art at the window.

"He might be sitting down the street right now, Art. Just out of sight."

"He might."

Red looked in both directions.

"Maybe it's time the mouse got some help from the other mice and put the cat on defense."

Art glanced at Red.

"What do you mean?"

"I could take Scotty and Bill with me. The three of us could follow him everywhere. Maybe after a while, he gets tired of it all and heads home."

Art pondered it. It was one way to go. He appreciated Red's loyalty. If Bedford really had no plan and was just jerking his chain—maybe. But what if Bedford had a gun? What about that? What if he was like his old man in that regard? A younger Brant Russell. Like father like son and all that. Besides, he couldn't allow others to stand in for him. He no longer wanted to be Chief—but he *was* Chief. The buck still stopped at his desk. It *was* still his desk, his title. Argus was still his responsibility. Red was learning fast, but Scotty and Bill were raw. Their lives were his responsibility. And this thing with Bedford, whatever it was, was between the two of them.

Art patted Red's shoulder.

"Thanks, Red. But no. You don't know what you might be walking into with him. He might panic, might do something crazy. He may be crazy. We don't know."

Art walked back to his desk but decided he didn't feel like sitting down. He leaned against an edge toward Red.

"My gut tells me Bedford might be about ready to talk. He's played cat and mouse maybe long enough, and now he's had his good look at me out at the dam. I'll make sure he runs into me and we'll settle whatever it is."

Red leaned against the wall.

"Art, do you think he wants to get even with you?"

Art picked up his holstered revolver and placed it on his hip, where it had rested for so many years.

"I certainly hope not. I've got dinner plans with Carolyn."

Twenty

Red and Art stood on the sidewalk in front of the police station. Traffic was light and they both looked around for Bedford's car. The sun had snuck behind clouds.

"It's okay to send someone out on a little scouting mission, Red, if you get my drift."

"I do get it. And I'll put Scotty on the road, too, to see if we can spot our boy."

Art nodded. He approved of the choice. Scotty was more experienced than Bill. Red seemed already to be making the decisions a Chief had to make.

"But no confrontations, Red."

"I'll make sure Scotty knows to just keep tabs. Scotty's pretty level-headed. I'll have him keep a discreet distance if he spots Bedford. No drama, no mess."

Good, Art thought. Red was seeing more of the bigger picture of the job every day.

"You have to be in town," Art said. "When I'm out, you run the show. Clear?"

"Very clear, Chief."

"You're first deputy, Red."

"I've got it, Chief."

"I know you do." Art slapped him lightly on the back. "I'll check in with you later."

"Okay, Chief. But you watch your back."

"Always."

Art drove back out to the dam and made his way home slowly, stopping to look up lanes and to check side roads, but he didn't see Bedford anywhere. He watched his rearview mirror—nothing. He wondered what the bastard did all day and where he ate and where he slept. Did he base himself out of Bloomington? That seemed the most likely choice. Much easier to hide over there. Well, while the cat's away, the mice will play, he thought, and then he scolded himself and reminded himself that Bedford was now properly the mouse and *he* was the cat. A big cat ready to pounce. Things had gone far enough.

As he drove, he was very aware of the gun on his hip. He felt off balance after not wearing it for so long. When he got home, he took it off and slid it under the front seat. He sat in the car in his driveway for a few moments, running over his sales pitch for Carolyn.

He found her sitting with an iced tea on the patio facing the lake. He sat in the chair next to her. She had a stack of student essays on her lap and was reading the first one. He glanced across the lake at the marina. Suddenly he felt quite self-conscious and nervous.

"There's more tea in the fridge, Art," she said without looking up.

He looked back over at the marina. A tiny speck of a boat had just pulled up alongside it, but the marina was too far away to make out the people.

"From the look of that stack of papers, you might need something stronger than tea," Art said.

She looked up and smiled.

"After the first few, scotch will definitely sound better than tea."

"I hear you on that." He looked again over at the marina. He knew he was just stalling. "When do you have to return those papers?"

"I've got some time. I thought I'd just do a few today, while my eyes were still sharp."

Art fidgeted in the chair.

"How about we drive over to Bloomington for dinner, Carolyn? Maybe that Italian place—Romano's."

"What's the occasion?" she said, still reading the first paper.

He knew better than to lie and claim it was just a spontaneous notion.

"Well, I've got an idea to run by you. Something interesting. And I want your take on it."

She looked up at him.

"We could do that here, over a couple scotches."

"Yeah, but there's no linguini in Alfredo sauce here. No Chianti. No waiter fussing over us."

"Do you need to be fussed over?"

"Tonight, I'd let you fuss me some."

"Down, big boy. Tell me what this big idea is about before any fussing can begin."

"I can tell you at Romano's."

"But I've got essays to grade."

He was ready for that one.

"But just a few for today, you said. Take them with you and you can do some on the drive over. You could even make yourself a scotch for the ride over."

"What would the police say about that?"

"I know a guy. Don't worry."

"So, you're thinking of everything, is that it?"

"Right now, I'm thinking about linguini in Alfredo sauce and a glass of Chianti and the smells from Romano's kitchen. You know—ambience."

"Ambience. And maybe some fussing later on?"

"That, too."

"Well, your fussing may just depend on how good or bad this idea of yours turns out to be. Art, can't you give me some hints?"

"It's something good, don't worry," Art said. "But something best suited for a jazzier atmosphere."

"Romano's is nice, but I wouldn't call it jazzy."

"But it beats McDonald's."

"True. But the food's cheaper here," she said. "So's the scotch."

"But you can't beat the service, Carol, and they wash the dishes and give us those little green mints on the way out. Now, how can you beat that?"

She studied his face a moment. He smiled, maintained eye contact. He knew that was a good idea. She smiled, too.

"Okay, Art. I'll go freshen up."

Over Chianti at Romano's, before the linguine in Alfredo sauce had even arrived, Art outlined his plan. As was his custom, he got to the heart of the matter.

"Babe, I want to buy the marina from Pete Armstrong." He leaned back in the booth, a little relieved that it was finally out and on the table. "I thought it might be best to just put it out there all at once."

Carolyn sipped her Chianti.

"The marina," she said softly. "Buy the marina."

"Yes." Art tried to gauge her reaction, but her face seemed neutral to him. "Pete will be ready to sell at the end of this season. By October, maybe November."

She curled her fingers around her glass but didn't pick it up. She moved it back and forth a couple times.

"You've talked to him about it?" she said.

"Yes. Earlier today I went over there. The deal includes the diner paying rent, which is a plus."

He could clearly see she was pondering it, speculating about the consequences, how it would affect their lives.

"And now *we're* talking about it," she said.

He nodded vigorously.

"Absolutely. I told Pete it would have to be a joint decision between us. We've always talked through our important decisions. Now I'm putting this one on the table for discussion."

"Did you make any commitment to Pete?"

He knew that was a test and potentially a trap if he wasn't careful.

"None, Carolyn. No way. I told Pete I was interested but would do nothing without you on board with it. He even asked me if I had run it by you."

Her face brightened, and he knew he had passed the test. He felt that she trusted him, but he also knew that she wanted to have her vote carry real weight.

"How much to buy it?"

"Close to two-hundred grand." Asking the price was a good sign, he felt. "That's a lot, I know."

She arched her eyebrows slightly, but then smiled.

"Goodness, Art. It's a fortune." She lifted her glass and sipped more Chianti. "Now tell me why it makes sense financially."

Good, he thought. *She's approaching it from the practical standpoint. She wants evidence. She's open to practical possibilities.*

"The marina sells all sorts of things, and the diner pays rent, but essentially, it's a floating gas station, and gas stations generate good income. Pete says revenues would pay the loan and clear a good amount over that monthly as income. If we kept it, say, ten years, we could sell and cash in a lot of equity—and the price will continue to improve over time. It's a heck of an investment. We make money from it now and a bunch later."

The waiter returned and left a basket of bread wrapped in a red cloth on the table. When he left, Carolyn opened the cloth and took a piece of bread. Art slid the butter dish toward her.

"Thanks," she said.

Art watched her butter the bread slowly. It smelled very good, and he was hungry. She took a large bite and then sat the bread down on a plate.

"I could live off this bread," she said. "So, how much down payment?"

Always on top of important details, he thought.

"Perhaps twenty-five percent, which we have in CDs. Which we would build back up while also having a good income from gas sales and diner rent. And we both have retirement plans. Down the road, we'll do pretty well, babe."

As *was* her custom, she found the real bottom line quickly.

"So, all this means you want out as Chief?"

"Yeah, babe. That's what it means all right. It's time. I'm ready for something else."

"The marina?"

"I believe so. I do feel it's a good move."

She nodded and started to drink but put the glass back down.

"But money aside, Art, and I do see how it's likely a good investment, but money and investment aside—why?"

The million-dollar question, he thought. He needed a million-dollar answer. He let his heart speak.

"Look, it's not just that I don't want to be Chief anymore. It's that I'm *not* Chief anymore. Not really. Not like even a year ago. Looking back, I see that taking off the uniform and gun were just steps toward taking off the badge, too I guess in a way I've been slowly shedding layers. Now I'm down to Art Millage and he's kind of worn out from having to always be strong and in control and looking out for the town. I'm about out of gas as Chief."

He sighed and felt he had gotten as close to who he was now as he could for the time being.

She slid her hand across the table and placed it on his.

"When it's time for change, it's time, Art. And only you can know when that is."

He felt great relief, like an ocean wave washing over him and cleansing him, the salt stripping him down, sanding him down, to the essential and unvarnished man—to Art. There were still plenty of details left: talking to the bank, setting a date and resigning, and getting Hedges behind the move to install Red as Chief. But Art felt like it was sort of official now. It was real. He would soon just be a private citizen again. For the first time in twenty-five years. It was thrilling and scary, too—as life should be, he thought.

Then he remembered Nathan Bedford. That one, last barrier before private life. It could likely not be avoided and would have to be handled, surmounted.

But he had burdened Carolyn with enough for one night. Nathan Bedford could wait for tomorrow. It was not his night.

This was Art's night.

After a moment Carolyn said, "Art, I need to ask. What does the marina mean to you? Besides an income, I mean."

It came to him clearly, immediately.

"Freedom."

Twenty-One

Art decided to use Maggie Thomas's place as bait for Nathan Bedford. He had no grand plan. It just came to him clearly that he needed to turn the tables on Bedford and confront him, find out what the man wanted, and to take his measure. There really might be nothing to the whole escapade except curiosity fueled by a little natural emotional anger over his father. But a father he never knew, apparently, and by Art's reasoning, that should impose a natural limit to the anger, the thirst for any boneheaded notion for revenge. Theoretically, anyway. If Bedford wasn't some nut job. Art knew that theories often did not survive first contact with reality.

The plan struck Art as being an awful lot like fishing: where the fish were could often be a mystery, and the fisherman resorted to trying different types of bait in different locations to entice the fish out into the open. Fish usually didn't just jump in the boat any more than Bedford was likely to knock on the police station door and politely ask if he could drop in for some of Red's strong coffee, though Art would welcome him if he did. That would be the civilized approach. But he was pretty sure the civilized approach wasn't going to happen. Just a gut feeling.

So, back to fishing as strategy: trolling was one method fishermen used. Dragging a baited line behind a moving boat could tempt fish to strike and that was what Art figured he had to do to coax Bedford out into the open, too. He had to think of Bedford as a fish he intended to reel in and dispose of.

Art sent Bill and Scotty outside of town to look for Bedford. He put Red on city streets, too. Their only task was to radio Art if they spotted him and then stay out of the way. It loomed as a test of sorts. If after twenty-five years as a cop he couldn't handle some errant boy on a foolish mission from Indiana, that would be a mighty poor legacy indeed. He slipped his gun and holster onto his belt. It felt uncomfortable, but he knew it was a wise decision. Art had to be ready for anything.

As he drove out of town, he understood that he no longer had the town's safety as his overriding concern. Now he thought of his wife, of his desire to buy the marina and live his life pleasantly and on his terms on the lake without a public image to maintain. Now he felt that he was working for himself for the first time. The town was his client only by association. He did not think that was wrong. It was just a fact. Life presented shifting loyalties.

It didn't take so long to spot Bedford. Red found his car in the lot at Bunnie's Tavern and Art doubled back to town and parked on the street in front of the lot but close to the corner so he wouldn't be spotted right away by anyone coming out the tavern door. The location was a bit sobering: behind Bunnie's, in the woods, was where he had killed Brant Russell. In the lot, near the front door to the tavern, was where he first saw Dominick on his back and bleeding, Jesse standing over him. Carolyn had been with Art that day. It had been their first real date. What a way to end a first date. They had gone to lunch in Bloomington—Romano's, in fact—and were returning when they passed Bunnie's and saw Dominick down, a man with a gun running around a corner. The rest, as they say, was history.

Go to lunch, woo a gal, and kill a guy.

Art sat there and wondered whether Bedford had walked behind the tavern to see where it all had happened. Why not? He had come all this way. Might as well get the whole enchilada. The newspaper article certainly described it all and specified where it happened. He had to know. So be it. It was just woods. Nothing at all to see. The boy had had his grand tour, but now it was time for Art to get on top of things.

Soon Red pulled alongside and rolled down his window.

"Red, I've got other plans for you."

"Shouldn't I stick with you?"

"No. Right now Roger Gilstrap would be right—we look like a cop convention out here. I want you to go around the block and pull into the alley where you can see Bunnie's. Someone would have to be looking pretty damn hard to see you sitting there. And Bedford won't. He'll see me once he comes out and looks around and that will be his focus."

"You're sure about that? Red said.

"Reasonably."

Red looked over toward the alley.

"Why am I going to the alley?"

"I want you to sit there and tell me if Bedford takes the bait."

"What are you going to do until then?"

"Not a thing. I'm going to sit right here and listen to the radio out of Bloomington and wait for the dipshit to come out the front door. When he does, I'm going to drive out to Maggie Thomas's place. You radio me to let me know he's following."

Red nodded.

"Okay, I've got it. And then I come, too?"

"No."

"But—"

"No buts, Red. I killed his old man and so I've inherited the son, too. Whatever he's up to, it's my duty to see about it."

"Okay. I'm with you."

"I know that."

"Art—why Maggie's?"

Art shrugged.

"It's as good a place as any for an ambush. I know the lay of the land pretty good there. Do some reading on Robert E. Lee—he knew how to judge a battlefield. Except at Gettysburg."

"We're calling it an ambush, Art?"

"An encounter. Just an encounter to meet Mr. Nathan Bedford. Now scoot over to the alley."

Red tapped his steering wheel with his fingers.

"You know, Art, maybe he's drinking in there and we could just bust him for that once he gets behind the wheel."

"Could be. I'll keep that in mind. Now scoot."

Red stared at Art a moment.

"Good luck—Chief."

Red pulled away and Art watched him round the corner in his rearview mirror.

Art found a classic rock station and listened to the Rolling Stones and then The Beatles. An old Beatles favorite came on: "A Day in the Life."

Bedford came out of Bunnie's a half hour later. He stopped just outside the door to light a cigarette. He didn't spot Art until he'd had a couple puffs on the cigarette and then he stared at Art, the cigarette dangling from a corner of his mouth. Art assessed him: stocky and muscular in a tight t-shirt and jeans. He wore sunglasses. His stance, legs wide apart, seemed a bit cocky, thought Art couldn't be sure about it.

Art wondered whether he could take the boy if it came to that—and it just might, he reminded himself. Art was in decent shape and had a couple inches of height over Bedford, presumably some reach, too. Reach could be crucial. He'd fought a little in the Navy—just boxing on his ship, but he knew how to find a chin with a quick jab followed by a hard right. The secret to a fight, he knew very well from growing up in Chicago, was not size or muscles. It was willingness. He'd seen plenty of studly men fall apart after the first punch. What was that saying? Not the size of the dog in the fight, but the size of the fight in the dog? Art had plenty of fight left in him, and this boy Bedford had started to annoy him. Bedford stood in the way of a life Art wanted.

Art pulled away from the curb and then punched the accelerator just enough to toss up loose gravel behind the car. A little statement for Mr. Bedford. A challenge. Art glanced over at the boy as he went by and then in his rear mirror caught sight of Bedford walking quickly to his car. Art had been very tempted to give him the finger, but that was too unprofessional. He was still Chief.

Outside of town, on the road to Maggie's place, he slowed down until he caught sight of Bedford's car well behind him in the mirror. The road was straight as a zipper out to Maggie's, except for one bend just before her house. That was all Art needed. It would put him out of sight just long enough.

When he reached Maggie's, he pulled up her lane and climbed out quickly. A cloud of dust kicked up by his car drifted over him. He sprinted across the road to a thick tree just on the other side. He peeked around the trunk down toward the bend, but Bedford had still not appeared. Good, he thought. Very damn good. I've got the drop on the boy.

He caught his breath and pulled his revolver and took another peek: Bedford was now coming through the bend slowly. Just before he reached the lane, Bedford slowed to a crawl and Art could clearly see the boy looking toward the house.

When Bedford reached the mouth of the lane, he stopped, and then Art stepped from behind the tree, the revolver pointed toward the ground, and walked right up to Bedford's window before the boy knew he was there.

"Put both hands on the wheel."

Bedford flinched slightly and turned his head enough to see Art and the gun. He slowly put his other hand on the steering wheel.

Staring straight ahead, Bedford said, "Nice move, Chief. Very smooth."

Art brought the revolver up and stepped closer for a look at the passenger seat, but it was empty.

"Now slowly," Art said, "I want you to put it in park and switch off the ignition."

Bedford did so and put his hand back on the wheel. Art stepped back and slightly toward the rear of the car, away from the door.

"Now slowly get out and face away from me with your hands behind your head," Art said.

He held the revolver up again for emphasis. Bedford got out and put his hands behind his head and Art patted him down. Satisfied he wasn't armed, he told Bedford to turn around.

"Should we be standing in the middle of the road, Chief?"

"Don't worry, son, it's a lonely old road. Not much traffic this time of day."

"So I see. Can I lower my arms now?"

"Slowly."

Art raised the revolver again. Over Bedford's shoulder he could see that Maggie had come outside and was standing on her porch watching.

Bedford seemed unsure what to with his lowered hands and he glanced several times at Art's revolver.

"Have you been drinking, son?" Art said, though he didn't think Bedford exhibited any signs of it.

Bedford shook his head.

"Just a Pepsi back at the tavern. And a roast beef sandwich. They have a pretty fair roast beef there, Chief. But you probably know that."

Art sensed that the boy could get under someone's skin pretty easily.

"We're not here to discuss the roast beef, Mr. Bedford."

"No, I suppose not."

Art lowered his gun.

"Son, what in good Christ do you think you're doing following me around like a lost puppy? Some might take that the wrong way. I didn't care for it myself."

"Curiosity," Bedford said after a pause.

"Curiosity and the cat," Art said. "Not a pretty story."

"Maybe, Chief. Maybe not."

Art didn't care for the answer. Was that a threat lurking inside it?

"Let's move on off this road," Art said. "Go on over to the house—slowly."

"What about my car?"

"It isn't your car," Art said. "Go on now, over by those trees in the yard."

"Okay, Chief. It's your party."

"I'm glad you grasp the obvious, Nathan."

Maggie had come down the steps of her porch and Art waved her to come over.

"Chief," Maggie said. "Looks like you've got some kind of handful here."

"Maggie, can you drive a car?"

"Why, what sort of question is that? Of course I can drive a car. I may be old, but I'm not senile."

"Sorry. Will you pull this fella's car up off the road for me?"

"I guess I could, Chief. Are you going to want me to wash it, too?"

"Parking will be fine, Maggie. I appreciate your help."

Art herded Bedford to the trees and had him sit on the grass. Maggie came back with the car keys and gave them to Art.

"We're going to borrow your yard for a bit here," Art said. "Will you give us some time? Go on back up to the porch, if you will."

"Things are just getting interesting, Chief," Maggie said. "But okay. I'll move along."

Bedford had his back against the trunk of a small tree.

After Maggie was back on her porch, Art said, "I know why you're here, Nathan."

"No mystery, I guess." Bedford glanced over at Maggie's house. "Nice place. I wouldn't mind living here myself."

"You don't have time for real estate shopping," Art said.

"Oh? How's that?"

"You're on the way back to Seymour, Indiana, Nathan. Back to your job, if you still have one."

"The factory's on a summer layoff right now, Chief. No job to go back to for a while."

"And there's no reason for you to be *here*."

Bedford cocked his head to the side.

"Except that it's a free country, Chief. Aren't you forgetting that one? Maybe I'd like to settle down in Argus. I've seen some cute girls around town."

Art holstered his revolver.

"Boy, you're on a fool's errand. Do you even know it?"

Bedford frowned and shook his head.

"Here I am, a law-abiding tourist spending money in your fair county, and you call me a fool. Not very hospitable, Chief."

"Let's cut to the chase, Nathan. What do you want from me?"

"I could ask *you* that, Chief. I'm the one under arrest here."

"You're not under arrest. We're having a conversation."

"You've got a gun."

"And I'm entitled to have it handy when the son of a man I had to shoot shows up and follows me everywhere."

Art watched Bedford's eyes narrow, but the boy managed not to lose his cool at the mention of his father. He looked away for a moment.

"You guess me to be a threat, Chief?"

"I never guess. I find out. You here to size me up, Nathan? Did you have a look behind Bunnie's, out in the woods? Did you actually do that? Go out there and walk around and look for the actual spot and all that?"

Bedford looked up at the Chief and for the first time Art saw that anger was open on his face.

"Yeah, I took a look," Bedford said. "It's a free country, like I said."

"It sure is, Nathan. You sure are right about that. Hey, I could take you back there right now, if you like. Want to go?"

Bedford looked at the ground.

"I don't reckon I do, no."

"Are you sure? Last chance, son. I'll drive you back there myself. I'll even help you find the exact damn spot. You could scoop up some dirt and take it back to Indiana. Would that appeal to you?"

"Not really," Bedford said softly. He pulled his legs up under his chin and placed his hands on his shins. "Now what?"

Art regretted the dirt remark immediately. It was cruel. But he had a job to do and decided it was better to be rough and maybe resolve the issue once and for all. No good could come of Bedford lingering and stewing about a man he never met, but apparently had developed some sense of allegiance to.

"Now what?" Art said. "You tell me. Look, Nathan—you never even knew your father. And son, I had no choice that day.

Believe me. Brant Russell—your father—fired at me. Do you understand what I'm telling you here? He tried to kill me—and he had just shot another man. I had no choice."

Bedford looked up at Art slowly. Art thought the look rather smug.

"We all have choices," Bedford said.

"Not as many as you might think, Nathan. When you get older, you'll see what I mean."

A car pulled up behind them in Maggie's lane and Art saw it was Red. He was actually glad Red had ignored his orders and showed up, but he wasn't entirely sure why.

"Reinforcements?" Bedford said when Red walked over to them.

"Everything okay, Chief?" Red said.

Bedford smirked.

"The Chief was just teaching me about choices."

"He's sure got a mouth on him," Red said.

"Go through his car, Red," Art said. "Top to bottom."

While Red searched the car, Art mulled what he knew about Bedford so far: not so damn much. The boy was feisty, arrogant, but didn't seem all that violent. That could be misleading, he knew. Sometimes that stayed hidden until too late. Calm waters could suddenly turn ugly and swamp a boat.

"Can I stand up now, Chief?" Bedford said.

Art thought about it a moment.

"Slowly."

"I know," Bedford said. "Everything gets done slowly around here."

"That's how we like things here, son. Nice and slow."

What a mouth, Art thought. That concerned him a little. He worried that Bedford could be the type who could talk himself into something and then right past the point of no return. He wasn't sure, but that impression of him was gaining traction.

Red closed the car trunk.

"It's clean, Chief."

"Thanks, Red. Okay, Nathan. It's time for you to hit the road. You've got some driving ahead of you to make it back to Indiana. Best get started."

Bedford looked at Red and then Art.

"That's it? Just like that?"

"We didn't have time to plan a going away party," Red said.

Nice one, Art thought.

"Deputy Foley here is going to escort you out to the interstate, Nathan. He'll make sure you get started off right."

"I'll be your tour guide," Red said.

"And if I was to come back?" Bedford said.

Art glared at him for a long moment.

"You have a nice trip home, son."

Twenty-Two

When Red got back to the station, Art was eager for his report and met him in the hallway when he heard heavy footsteps coming. *Those squeaky, sagging floorboards,* Art thought. *When Red is Chief, he really ought to look into getting them fixed.*

"How'd it go, Red?"

"Smooth as a baby's bottom. I followed him all the way out and even got on the interstate with him for a few miles, just to let him know I was still there."

Art nodded solemnly and thought about the chances Bedford really was gone.

"You think he's still headed home?"

"I'll think that if you will."

Art smiled.

"I hear you. No real way to know at this point."

"Unless he suddenly parks out front," Red said.

"Yeah, that would be a dead giveaway."

"But I can call that Seymour chief, Art. He could let us know that Bedford made it home."

"*If* he makes it home."

"He just might, Art. You might have put the fear of Jesus in him."

"Jesus wouldn't have needed to use fear."

"A little fear can't hurt in these things," Red said.

Art nodded.

"Okay, give that Seymour chief a call. And let him know we appreciate all the help."

Red turned and started off, then stopped. Art knew what was coming. He'd already thought it.

"Art, what if he just turns off somewhere down the road and works his way back? What then?"

"Plan B, I guess."

"What *is* Plan B?"

"Damned if I know. I'm still pulling for Plan A."

"Maybe we could arrest him," Red said.

"For what?"

Red shrugged.

"Maybe for coming back when you instructed him to leave. I don't know, disturbing the peace—resisting an officer?"

"Maybe littering, too?" Art said. "Can we really arrest him for any of that? And make something stick in court, that is?"

"I'm not real sure."

"Neither am I." Art sighed, turned back toward his office. "It's always a good idea to be sure when you arrest someone, Red. Makes life a whole lot easier."

Art drove out to the marina. He found Pete next door at the diner, sitting on a stool at the counter.

"Warm day, Chief. But the iced tea is nice and cold here."

Art ordered iced tea and sat next to Pete.

"How's your day been?"

"Slow. And boring. Or I wouldn't be here guzzling tea. How about yours, Chief?"

"Not so slow, not so boring."

The waitress, a young blonde girl, brought Art's tea. It was very cold and delicious, with just a dash of sugar and a splash of lemon. "You keep forgetting to call me Art, Pete."

"I reckon I do."

"And you'll need to call me Art instead of Chief if we're going to do some business together."

Pete swiveled his stool toward Art.

"You spoke to Carolyn, did you?"

"I did. And she's on board with the deal. Still ready to sell to a soon-to-be ex-cop?"

Pete grinned.

"I'd be tempted to sell to an ex-anything, I reckon. But I'm glad I'm selling to you. It does matter who takes over out here."

They shook hands.

"Been to the bank yet, Art?"

"I called Kent Rieger over there and set something up for this week."

"Good," Pete said. "I doubt you'll have any trouble getting them to back you."

"Kent did say it sounds pretty doable."

Pete sipped his tea. Art glanced at the menu, uncertain whether he wanted to eat or not. He was still a little unsettled after all the Bedford business.

"When do you step down as Chief?"

Art put down the menu, decided he would eat at home.

"I haven't decided yet, for sure. Before the year's out, though, I suspect. Maybe by November. Before Christmas."

"Who knows about it?"

"Now *you* do. And Carolyn. That's it."

"What about your men?"

"No, I haven't told them yet."

"I can keep it under my hat a while," Pete said. "Until you're ready to announce it."

Art realized he needed to write a letter of resignation and set an effective date. Hedges would need that. The sooner the better, he figured. In the morning he would give Hedges something and have the date. November something sounded about right. After fifteen years as Chief he couldn't see himself just giving two weeks' notice and then disappearing as though he worked at Kmart. And he needed a little more time to make sure Red was ready to at least run things in an interim.

"I don't know, Pete—if you want to give Caitlin Rutherford a thrill, tell her I'm quitting the next time she drives up for gas. She won't be sorry to see me go."

Pete chuckled.

"And when I move down to Florida, I won't be sorry to lose her as a customer."

They clinked their glasses together, and Art had a thought that amused him.

"I hadn't thought this out, but next season, Caitlin will have to come to me to fill up her boat."

"There you go," Pete said. "And then some of her dollars will be going in your pockets."

"I like the irony."

Pete finished his tea.

"How about the nickel tour of the marina?"

"I'd like that," Art said. "Lead the way."

After nearly two hours with Pete going over how to handle gas deliveries and keep the pumps in good running order, Art drove home. He was tired. It had been a long day and confronting Bedford had taken more out of him than he had realized at first. Carolyn was already home and grading some essays. He was hungry, but wanted to sit first, maybe sip a scotch, and decompress. He made himself a Laphroaig on the rocks and sat in a lawn chair down by the little dock and watched ducks bobbing on the bay.

Art wasn't pleased with how he had handled Bedford. In retrospect it seemed a bit ham-handed to him. He might have kept his gun holstered, for one thing. He had been harsh and even a bit cruel with the remark about scooping up dirt from where Russell had died. That was out of line. The boy didn't deserve that. He had really come on a bit like some old, tough Southern sheriff in a movie—a little too much like Rod Steiger in *In the Heat of the Night*, he thought. He cringed a little at the image, and when he had finished his drink, he walked back to the house for a second one.

As he made his drink, he looked out the kitchen window and saw Red drive up and he stiffened a little. He took the drink with him out the back door to the driveway. Red didn't look to be concerned about anything as he walked up the driveway, Art thought, and so he hoped that was a good sign.

"Red, what's up?"

Red smiled broadly.

"Good news. Bedford's back in Indiana. The Seymour chief confirmed it."

Art sipped his scotch and felt relieved. He still wasn't happy about how he had handled it, but the results pleased him.

"That's very damn good. That's what we wanted."

"You sent him packing, Art."

Art winced slightly.

"Or maybe he saw the light on his own."

"Well, whatever it was, he's gone," Red said. "That's what counts. I thought you'd appreciate hearing it in person."

"I do, Red. I really do. That's good work."

"You're not mad I went on out to Maggie's after you?"

"No. There's a time for sidestepping orders and backing up the Chief, I reckon. You did the right thing. I was being a little overly protective, I guess."

Red smiled broadly and seemed to stand straighter.

"Red, do you want a drink? Scotch? Or a beer?"

"I'm still on the clock."

"Yeah, you are. I should know better. But you're off tomorrow, Red. Can you come by for a drink in the late afternoon? There's something important to go over."

"About Bedford?"

"No. Something else. I want your view on some things. But tomorrow. Late afternoon, before dinner."

"Okay. Sure, Art. I'll see you then."

Art watched him leave and sipped his scotch. It was getting dark. He glanced at the sky. Several bats climbed and banked sharply above him. Tomorrow he would tell Red he intended to back him as Chief—as his successor. But tonight, Art didn't mind if he got himself a little drunk.

Twenty-Three

Art woke up mid-morning with a mild hangover, but the good news about Bedford, combined with a big breakfast of ham and eggs and toast and coffee helped wash it away. Carolyn had left a note saying she had gone shopping in Bloomington with Iris Cochrane, a social studies teacher at the high school. After breakfast and when he was more awake, he recalled that the trip had been planned for some time.

He showered, put on shorts, t-shirt and flip-flops, and fired up the boat. He sped south toward the dam and thought of fishing in one of the quiet southern bays but decided he wanted to be on the water without working too hard so he could just think and feel the gentle waves rocking him as he drifted.

He cut the engine at the mouth of one of the bays opposite the dam. No need to get into the dam current. He had put a good amount of distance between himself and the dam. Art sat on the back of the driver's seat so that he had a better look at the greenish-blue water around him. If it had been afternoon, a cold beer would be tempting, but Art didn't want to get into the habit of drinking of a morning just because it was a day off and he was on the lake.

The new area conservation officer, Billy Teague, was on the lake, and he pulled alongside Art. Billy was mid-thirties with a shock of black hair, a boyish round face, and an eager attitude. The longtime officer had abruptly retired, and Billy was transferred down from an area north of Bloomington. Billy had tied up at Art's dock the first week on the job to introduce himself. Professional courtesy.

"Day off, Chief?"

"Every day on a lake is a day off, Billy. How's the world of water crime?"

"Slow. The weekend is starting off a bit slower than I expected for a lake this size. But a while ago I did send some kids back to shore to get life preservers."

"No tickets today?"

"Naw. It was just a bunch of jerky kids. Why bother? They came back and showed me the jackets. Lesson learned. Safety preserved after all."

Art nodded approval.

"That's the way to look at it. Some things just aren't worth a fuss."

He thought of Bedford. Had he made too much of a fuss there? Likely. He had gotten a little emotional. And it would have been so much better without that damn dirt remark.

"I hear you about making a fuss," Billy said. "So, just out here drifting today, Chief? Some R and R?"

"That's right. Just drifting. Just going with the flow, as they say."

Billy looked north toward the causeway and then southwest toward the dam.

"Well, so far, it's a good day to go with the flow. Not enough traffic to amount to much. But be watchful. When more kids hit the lake, the traffic patterns and manners can sometimes get shot all to hell. Last week, I found a guy out here taking a nap. Can you believe it? Sound asleep, for God's sake. He was lucky it was midweek and almost no traffic, but still, that's a dicey thing to do."

Art smiled.

"That's good advice. I appreciate it. I promise not to nap. Just doing some thinking."

Billy slipped a Styrofoam fender between the two boats to keep them from rubbing hulls.

"What do you think about, Chief? If you don't mind that I ask, that is."

Art shrugged.

"I don't mind. Just clearing my head, really. Being on the lake is good for that. It's quieter out here."

Billy looked north, at a boat that had just emerged from under the causeway.

"Later in the afternoon it will be a madhouse out here. You were smart to come out early. I get a lot busier in the afternoon, for sure. And if there's alcohol involved, it can get challenging, to say the least."

Art realized that Billy must have wanted some shop talk of sorts—some camaraderie, perhaps. He worked mostly alone, except busy holidays when the state would pair him with a second officer and even a second boat. But most of the time, he worked alone. Art saw Billy, like Red, too, as a version of himself long gone. A phantom from the past.

It was sort of like talking to himself from the past, from the early days.

"Billy, how do you handle it when someone's drinking too much out here?"

"Carefully. Very carefully. Driving a car and drinking is just wrong—but out here, plenty of folks feel entitled to have a beer or two on their boats. They feel like the lake is their backyard. Like an extension of their backyard. And they don't think they are doing anything wrong or hurting anyone. I understand that. I really do. But when there's a boating accident, booze is almost always a factor."

Art nodded but remembered when he and Carolyn had drunk as they cruised one night. And he knew they would again. With no remorse.

"How much leeway do you give folks out here?" Art said. "With alcohol, I mean."

"Plenty, really. I'm just one man, Chief."

"Call me Art."

"Okay—Art. Like I was saying, I can't bust everyone. I don't try. I have to be on the lookout for the ones who look like trouble waiting for a place to happen. And if it gets rough, I call the county sheriff for backup. Sometimes, though, I can talk the folks who are a bit tipsy into taking the party back to shore. I'll settle for that and call it a win."

"You fight the fights you can win," Art said. "You save the people you can save. Then you go home and learn how to sleep at night."

Billy grinned.

"Good advice, Art. You just make that one up?"

"No, that one comes from an old partner I had up in Chicago. When I was your age. A long time ago. Another time, another universe, really."

"Maybe it was another time, but what cops face—pretty universal."

"And timeless," Art said.

"Absolutely. That's a fact. Well, time to roll, Art. Good to see you again."

"You take care, Billy."

"I'll take it any way I can get it."

"There you go."

Billy offered a hand and they shook. Billy started his boat and slowly cruised away until he could open the throttle without sending too much wake back at Art. Art watched Billy's boat grow small and then disappear under the causeway into the northern portion of Lake Argus. He wondered how long Red and Billy would last as cops. Would they last as long as he had? Maybe so. Maybe much longer. It was a tough life in so many ways, though. It was an image that was hard to live up to. He hoped they had what it takes. He was pretty sure he was tapped out in that department. Running on fumes, as the saying went. Running on empty.

His boat had drifted close to shore and Art assembled the spinning rod from the gunwale and tied a Mepps spinner on and cast it toward shore for a while. He caught several crappies, and then a bass, but let them all go. They all fought very well, but they were all rather small, and he wished them time to grow.

Late in the afternoon Red showed up in jeans and a Cubs t-shirt and Art realized how little he ever saw of Red out of uniform. It did sort of put Red into a new perspective. The boy looked younger in civilian clothes. Slightly smaller, too. He looked like he could be a student over at ISU. It made Art wonder how people were now viewing him, too, with the Chief uniform long a convention of the past.

Art greeted Red with a couple cold PBRs. He didn't figure Red for a scotch man and he was right. They sat in lawn chairs down by the dock.

"How's that girl of yours, Red? How's Mary?"

"She's doing fine. The bank moved her up to head teller. She gets a raise, too."

"Sounds like a banking career there," Art said. "That's good. That's a good field to be in. That's where the money is—literally. Just ask Willie Sutton."

"Who's Willie Sutton?"

"A famous bank robber. I thought you said you were reading more history."

"I guess I haven't gotten to Willie Sutton yet. What was *his* story?"

"Folks asked Sutton why he robbed banks. He said, that's where the money is."

Red chuckled.

"That's a good line. Mary finishes her degree at ISU in a year. That opens the door to management, with her experience. Legalized robbery."

"Maybe you should marry her," Art said. "When she gets to be bank president, you can retire and live on easy street."

"I thought you advised me to avoid marriage."

"Only if a guy isn't ready. But circumstances can make a man ready for something like that."

"What circumstances?"

"Things change in life, Red. Sometimes abruptly. You have to be ready for the changes and adjust—adapt."

"I'm not getting your drift here, Art."

Art sat his beer down.

"Well, now's one of those times when circumstances shift. And it affects you. I've decided to step down as Chief."

Art watched Red's eyes widen as the news sunk in.

"When?"

"Soon, Red. Before the year's out. It's time."

"Damn," Red said. "I had no idea. You're sure?"

"Yes. Very sure. I've had fifteen years as Chief. Ten before that in Chicago. Twenty-five years is enough for me."

Red sipped his beer.

"Did you know this was coming when you stopped wearing your uniform?"

Art took a drink and mulled it.

"I guess I did. It's been building for some time. But I don't think it was as clear-cut then as it is now."

"What will you do?" Red said. "You're still young."

"I'm buying the marina from Pete Armstrong. I'm going to run it and be a beach bum, I guess. But it's a good investment."

"No shit? The marina? When did all this come about?"

"Just the other day. Like I said, circumstances can change pretty fast. They dictate your future. They toss little curves here and there and you have to be ready for them."

"Damn," Red said. "This is huge."

"And here's the other thing, Red—I'm backing you to replace me as Chief. It's an opportunity for you, son."

"Jesus." Red looked off at the lake, then back at Art. "I'm honored. Surprised, too, but thanks."

"Why are you surprised?"

"You kid me all the time. I didn't think you took me seriously."

"I never kid anyone I don't like. But no more kidding. This is serious business."

"I guess so."

"I'll back you to Hedges, and that will get the council in line, too. Then it's up to you to handle it, my friend, and impress Hedges—if you want to keep the job."

"I do," Red said quietly. "Am I really ready for it?"

"You've learned a lot in the past five years. And Bill and Scotty respect you. That's important. They look up to you. That's a good start for a Chief, the respect of his men. That will be the selling point with Hedges and the council."

Red nodded gravely. His face, Art thought, managed to be a cross between earnestness and bewilderment. Red shifted his beer from hand to hand a couple times and then sat it down. He offered his hand and they shook vigorously, both of them grinning.

"It's a big step, Red. Absolutely. But you can do it, son. I mean that. But watch against being impulsive. Analyze things before jumping in whenever you can. Bill and Scotty will support you. Keep them involved in decisions. Don't isolate yourself."

"I won't." Red sighed heavily. "So, what now?"

Art grinned and slapped Red's shoulder.

"Now I think we drink another beer."

Twenty-Four

After the weekend, Art pitched into the loose ends: he gave Hedges Sullivan his letter of resignation, effective at the end of October. That was a sobering moment. Just a few more months as Chief. A quiet transition, he hoped. But he knew that Hedges liked Red and was receptive to him as Art's successor. That and that old chit Art held on the philandering mayor, who saw in a new Chief someone who didn't hold anything over him.

What was funny, Art thought, was how unlikely it would have been for him to ever use that chit. To actually cash it, that is. He would have never actually gone to Hedge's wife. The thought of doing so, of stepping into the middle of someone's marriage, disgusted him. It was all bluff. Fifteen years of bluff. Fifteen years of Hedges as a reliable ally because of a bluff. Life could be funny and a bit silly.

Kent Rieger at the bank agreed to loan Art the money as expected and a closing date on the marina sale was set. Pete Armstrong intended to see it through the season and help Art shut it down until the following March. Art had become an entrepreneur. It excited him but scared him, too.

Art took Red, Scotty, and Bill to lunch at Cameron's Café. Art thought it was likely the last time they would assemble publicly as a force under his command. It was an awfully bittersweet moment, but he kept reminding himself of his life yet to come.

Hedges came by and took a picture. Art reminded Hedges twice that he really wanted a copy. Bill and Scotty congratulated Red and thanked Art profusely for taking a chance and hiring them with no real experience. They were clearly relieved to know Red would take over instead of a stranger. Art managed to fight back tears and was misty-eyed for a few minutes.

"I thought I might be doing this job another five years," Art told them. "Twenty's often the milestone. But people have to know when it's time to turn a page. That time has come."

His deputies glanced among themselves to see who would speak first.

"We'll sure miss you, Chief," Scotty finally said.

"We will," Bill said. "We learned a lot from you."

"I'll still see you boys around," Art said. "And you can all come out and we'll go fishing some time."

"Sounds like a plan, Chief," Bill said.

"Call me Art, Bill. The Chief's days are numbered."

"But not forgotten," Scotty said.

"That's right," Bill added. He raised his water glass. "To the Chief—to Art."

One by one, they clinked their glasses with Art's. He was moved. He couldn't think of three men he would have rather had as deputies.

"Thanks, boys. I mean it—thanks a lot. I'm honored to have served with you. But soon it will be Red's time. He'll steer you right. Be there for him."

Red looked down at his plate.

"But big shoes to fill, Art," he said. "I'll do my best."

"They're not so big," Art said. "I'm just a man. Maybe that's the best advice I can give all of you—we're just men. It's useful to remember that when you're wearing the uniform and carrying the gun."

On the way home Art glanced at his watch. Carolyn wouldn't be home for an hour or so. Maggie's house was just ahead, and he impulsively turned up her lane. She was sitting on the porch but got up and met him at the bottom of the steps with her hands on her hips.

"How are you today, Maggie?"

"Well, now, I don't rightly know. Should I brace for trouble, Chief?"

Art smiled. Maggie always got right to the heart of matters. He liked that quality in people.

"No—no trouble today. Thought I'd stop on the way home and see how you're doing."

"Doing fine, Chief. But now you can explain to me what all that fuss was about the other day."

"Better start calling me Art, Maggie. I handed in my resignation today."

"Oh? What happened?"

"Nothing happened. I just reached the end of it, that's all. Time to move on."

"To what?"

"I bought the lake marina from Pete Armstrong. I aim to run it a few years."

"Well, I'll be," she said. "Ain't that something. That calls for a cold beer, don't you think?"

"I'd love one."

Art sat in the porch swing. Maggie brought two cold PBRs.

"But first tell me about this fella whose car I moved for you the other day. What in tarnation was that all about? And I saw that you ended up letting him go."

"I had to." Art took a sip. "No real laws broken. Just etiquette."

"Then who was he?"

Art put the beer in his other hand. The can was very cold and wet.

"He was a ghost. You and I have talked about ghosts."

"Yes, we have. But that fella was flesh and blood. When he left, Red followed him. That was no ghost."

"No, he sure wasn't. Just in a manner of speaking. You recall the shooting when I first became Chief? It was 1970. Fifteen years ago."

"I read it in the paper. What did that young feller have to do with it?"

"Not a thing. But he's the son of the man I shot back then. The man I killed."

"Mercy," she said. "My word, Art. Did he come over here looking for trouble?"

Art shrugged.

"I guess only he can answer that one. He followed me around a while. Then we sent him home. Back to Indiana."

"And he went?"

Art nodded and sipped more beer.

"That's what we hear from Indiana, anyway."

"And he never said what was on his mind?"

"Not really."

Art thought a moment. Was there anything about that day he had missed or overlooked? But he couldn't come up with anything. Nathan Bedford hadn't revealed much. Not anything Art could peek inside of, anyway.

"Pretty odd, Art, if you ask me."

"He was curious, I guess. We learned he'd never met his father. He was only about eight when it happened."

"Yet he showed up all these years later."

"In his shoes, I might be curious enough to have a look, too."

"You can't never tell about people," she said. "The loud ones are often just hot air, and the quiet ones, sometimes they explode."

"Let him explode over in Indiana."

"You don't mean that."

"No, of course not. I don't."

"Just put it behind you," she said. "How's your beer?"

"Cold. How come your beer is always colder than at Bunnie's?"

"I don't know. I guess it just is."

"That's life," Art said after another sip. "Sometimes it just is."

Fall

Twenty-Five

By the first days of September, it seemed apparent that fall would come early. Art thought he could feel it in the air. A whisper of things unseen but approaching. It had gotten a little cooler than usual, too. It was only a few degrees and subtle, but noticeable.

Art had fallen into a routine of going into town in the early mornings but returning to the lake by noon. One foot in, one foot out, as he viewed it. He was also gradually ceding more and more of center stage to Red, which was why he would go home by noon. He had little more than a month left as Chief and he now saw himself as mostly an adviser to Red, who was benefitting from not having to take over all at once.

On this day, he drove home and changed into jeans and a long-sleeve t-shirt and drove his boat across the lake to the marina. He would close on the property at the end of October, as Pete Armstrong finished out the season. Instead of tying up at one of the dock slips, he idled just outside the buoys and studied the marina from that distance. He was careful to stay out of the traffic pattern of boats approaching for fuel. There was a system of approach most boaters followed and understood. On busy days—weekends—there could be a dozen boats idling just inside the buoys, waiting their turn to pull alongside the marina wharf. Three boats could fuel at the same time and Pete had advised Art to help the pump jockeys direct traffic on the busy days to avoid collisions and frayed tempers. In retirement, he would be a traffic cop, Art thought with great amusement.

From the water, the marina was not particularly impressive as a building, he noted. The marina building itself was perhaps a little larger than a double-car garage. It had a cash register, soda machines, and supplies for sale, such as ice, a few groceries, and boating accessories. The wharf itself was old and splintered in places, and Pete had promised to help with repairs before he left.

But soon the whole thing would belong to Art. And the bank, of course. He was thrilled, actually. He had worked all his life for others: in the Navy, as a beat cop in Chicago, for Argus. He had never run a business, though he speculated that running a police force wasn't a bad background for a newly-minted entrepreneur. In fifteen years as Chief, he had dealt with all manner of human foibles, and he felt pretty damn seasoned. He had learned patience and believed that would be a strong asset in running the marina.

He saw Pete on the wharf in a conversation with one of the boys he hired each summer. A boat was approaching the dock for gas. He thought of going on in to say hello, but Pete looked busy and Art would just be a distraction. Here he was easing out as Chief, and easing in as owner of a business, and in both cases, at least for a while longer, he was something of a distraction to everyone. He was sort of temporarily out of focus. He was Chief now only in name and an owner in waiting. A curious limbo. It wasn't an uneasy feeling necessarily, just—awkward.

Art thought about how different things would be soon when he walked among people. He would no longer be a cop. The identity of a quarter century would be another layer cast aside. For a time, some people would certainly associate him with being Chief. Some people would probably always call him Chief. He wouldn't mind that. Not at all. At that point, it would be a term of honor and respect. It would be a courtesy title, and he would not carry the burden of *being* Chief. Like retired military. Like a retired general.

He wondered how Carolyn would view him. Would that change? An odd thought. He didn't see why it should change at all, but he knew that major changes had consequences. A ripple effect that one could not fathom at the time of the actual change. You had to wait for the ripples to play out and dissipate and see where you were then. Like waves generated at the center of the lake and slowly rolling toward shore.

Still, he pondered the past and what the circumstances had been when he and Carolyn had married. He had been eager to be the Chief back then, despite what had happened with Brant Russell. He supposed that back then he had even been comfortable with the public image, the uniform, the fact that he could not shed being Chief, even had he stripped naked. Was he actually worried she might somehow see him as less of a man now? It crossed his mind, though he felt that what existed between the two of them was very solid and built on mutual respect and acceptance. Their identities, the ones that made up their cores, were well-established and would endure. She would not always be a teacher, but she would always be Carolyn. He would always be Art.

He pushed the throttle forward and sped south. As he approached the dam, he swung the boat into a slow turn at full throttle and enjoyed the mild g-forces pushing on him as he completed the turn and roared along just yards off shore, but he knew the water was deep enough there and no one was fishing. Over his shoulder he saw his wake cascading toward shore and crashing with clouds of spray on the rocks. There was the ripple effect in practice. He eased the throttle back slowly until the bow had settled back to an idling waterline. He cruised along shore a while, sometimes seeing muskrats swimming and fish broaching the surface. He passed a tree that had fallen into the water: three turtles sitting on a large branch slipped into the water one by one.

Twenty-Six

Art decided to visit Dr. Holden one more time. It was an abrupt decision. He wasn't sure what he wanted from it. Closure? Perhaps. Closure to what? His career? Brant Russell? Margo Townsend? He felt he had mostly closed the book on Margo in Chicago. The Russell wound had been re-opened by Bedford, but he felt he was slowly healing again. He had learned to accept that he had done his duty that day. Both days. No, it was his career he felt like talking about. And the future. He still felt like he had a foot in both.

"Chief Millage," Walt said. "Come on in. Please, sit down."

"Thanks. Thanks for seeing me again on short notice. I seem to make a habit of that."

"Glad to. What's been going on since we last chatted?"

"I resigned as Chief. That's probably a good place to start."

Walt leaned back in his chair.

"Well, Art. That *is* news. Tell me about that."

"Are you surprised?" Art said with a sigh.

Walt crossed his arms over his chest and rubbed a thumb under his chin absently.

"I can't say I am, though I didn't predict it, either. We had only talked once. I guess I'm not surprised because you mentioned last time you wouldn't use your gun again."

"Couldn't."

Walt shrugged.

"Couldn't and wouldn't are kissing cousins in a messy family."

"You think it's purely a choice?"

"Yes. You chose to take it off, to no longer wear it, like the uniform."

"Just like that?"

"Yes. They're symbols of acts that repel you. Because you came to me having already shed the gun and uniform, I'm not surprised today to hear you quit. They were steps in a process. It takes some people years or decades to complete the process. For some, mere months."

Art smiled slightly. Walt was pretty smart. He might make a good cop.

"And so here I am," Art said.

"Here you are." Walt frowned. "Let me ask you this—where do you keep your gun, Art? Where is it now?"

"In a desk drawer at the station. Why?"

"Is it loaded?"

"No."

"Do you feel immune from danger now that you have resigned?"

"Next month I'm no longer Chief. No use for a gun after that. No real use now."

"I see."

"Do you?"

Walt grinned but didn't say anything. Art glanced around the room. It still had that vaguely antiseptic smell he recalled from the first visit.

"You sidestepped the question, Art."

"So I did. What do you want to know?"

"Do you feel immune to danger now, now that you're quitting?"

Art mulled it.

"No one is immune from danger. That's impossible. But I feel okay. Like I said, soon a gun will be irrelevant. That's the best I've got for you, Walt."

"That's perhaps not quite how to view it. It ought to be about what's best for you, not me."

Art knew that was true. He had become too glib.

"I'm not immune, Walt. Maybe I retired the gun early. I'm eager for private life. How's that?"

"More honest. So, what are your plans now? What comes next?"

"I'm buying the marina on Lake Argus. Planning to make a go of that."

"Good for you. How exciting." Walt nodded. "Running a business is a pretty different world than being a police chief."

"I'm ready for a new world. A different world."

"Who are you in this new world? How do you see yourself now, Art?"

That was the hard part, Art realized. He had been trying to make sense of it. He knew there were conflicting forces at work. On the one hand, he was very proud to have endured twenty-five years as a cop. It was an amazing record, really. But he could no longer be one and needed to know what his new identity was. Maybe he just needed more time to discover himself and feel comfortable. But he valued clarity and the lack of it worried him.

"I'm not always sure. Some days it's clear enough."

"And other days?"

Art ran a hand through his hair, which had grown a little longer, and brushed the collar of his shirt.

"And some days I'm a guy about to go work for himself for the first time in his life. That's exciting, and a little scary, too— but mostly exciting. I have few doubts about that decision. Some days, though, I'm a former cop, with all that experience, those skills, that mindset, and it's not always easy to just drop them, cast them aside. They say once a Marine, always a Marine. I think that's true to a degree for cops."

Walt leaned forward.

"I think that would be true for a psychiatrist, too."

"Really?"

"Absolutely. If I were to leave this practice and buy a business, part of me would always still be a shrink. Part of me would always be assessing people pretty critically. We have that in common, really. As necessary parts of our jobs, we have to get a good handle on who people are, why they do what they do."

Walt leaned back in his chair. Art respected him well enough, but knew the man enjoyed the sound of his own voice.

"Are you saying this is all sort of, like, natural feelings?" Art said.

"It is. Doubt is a natural part of the process of decision."

"I see," Art said, thinking he'd try the phrase, too. All in all, he was realizing this was a conversation he needed to have with Carolyn, and he was a little perturbed at himself for not doing it sooner. Walt was smart and useful, but a bit too clinical.

"Walt, do you think God will forgive me for my sins? For the killings?"

"I'm the wrong guy to ask. I can give you the names of some ministers, though."

"That's okay. I know a couple."

"Can you talk to them?"

"Only in riddles." Art managed a smile. Walt nodded, but grinned, too.

"I suspect God will make an accommodation, Art. But maybe the best thing to do is forgive yourself."

Art nodded.

"I see."

Art drove home and made ham and cheese sandwiches for lunch and then did something he did not usually do: he took a nap. He plopped on a couch, thinking he might read a new book he'd bought about Antietam, where Lee had been greatly outnumbered and had nearly been undone but had been saved at the last minute by A.P. Hill. Art discovered he was not yet ready to read it and put it down and fell asleep quickly.

In his dream, all seemed very well indeed. The sun shone brightly over Lake Argus, whose surface was smooth as glass. It was warm, but not hot, and he sat in a lawn chair on the marina wharf, looking out over the lake. He wore a Bears cap, a blue sleeveless t-shirt, khaki shorts and flip-flops. He could smell the

Coppertone lotion on his arms, legs, and face. His beach bum gear, he called it.

It was midweek, a slow time, and the only activity on the lake was a solitary sailboat with a red sail plying shore across the lake. It was so quiet that when a fish jumped in the expanse between the wharf and safety buoys, the sound was sharp and carried. Art could clearly see the fish's white belly as sparkling water cascaded off it. It was all a pleasant slow-motion.

Gulls chattered from the marina roof and one even swooped down to perch atop one of the gas pumps. It eyed Art curiously before flying off and taking position atop one of the safety buoys. An old Chevy Bel-Aire slowly crossed the long and narrow white causeway toward Argus. The day was very dry, and Art could see the white dust kicked up when the car tires hit loose rock along the road's shoulder. Art watched the car until it disappeared around the bend into trees on the far shore.

No boats had approached the wharf in hours. Art was content to feel the sun on his thighs and arms and watch the gulls squawking about something in the water. He was tempted to retrieve a fishing rod from inside the marina and cast a line to see if he might eventually snag a channel cat, but he didn't really want to get up and so he settled more into his chair.

He could see his house, a distant speck across the lake. He had erected a flagpole next to it and just for laughs had run up the Jolly Roger. Carolyn had thought it a bit tacky but said she didn't have to look at it and if it made Art happy she would make peace with it. He picked up the binoculars at his feet and looked at the flag. There was no breeze, and it hung limply and was a great disappointment.

After some time, Art detected a boat on the horizon coming down from the uppermost portion of the lake. Even with the binoculars, the boat was still mostly a moving speck. It was not at full-throttle, perhaps half at most, and it would be some time before it reached center lake and Art might identify it. It was not unusual mid-week to see a slow-moving boat as someone enjoyed the calm waters and cruised. Or maybe it was a fisherman idling slowly as he decided which of the upper bays to enter.

A breeze did finally come up, and the buoys began to bounce and plunge a little. Art slipped off his cap and let the air ruffle his hair, which had gotten longer still. The breeze rippled the lake just enough for Art to hear water lap gently and pleasantly at the shore beneath the wharf.

Art looked back out at the boat. It had come closer to center lake but was still too far away from him to make out who was in it. With the binoculars he could only see a tiny dark-clad figure sitting at the wheel. He wondered if the boat would come for gas. That was his business now, and he reminded himself to think like a businessman, though he really didn't want to have to leave his chair. He briefly regretted having given the day off to one of his crew, but on slow days he did his best to relieve them.

He watched the boat idling in center lake. He could see it was an inboard-outboard tri-hull. An Evinrude, perhaps. The big Evinrudes essentially had car engines and were powerful. Full-throttle from a still start would make the bow rise high and fall with a hard splash. He had driven one of the new ones when a local dealer had brought it out for trials. He watched this one make a lazy turn toward the far shore at half-throttle.

Art lost track of the tri-hull and listened as a pair of ducks sailed under the wharf. He heard their quacking, and it amused him. He waited and listened for the sound of lapping water to slightly increase below the wharf. That would be the subtle ripple effect from the tri-hull's turn at center lake. Soon he heard it and was pleased that he seemed so perceptive about such subtle matters.

He had not seen a person all morning. No one had walked onto the wharf looking for directions or wanting to buy anything from the marina. That could change at any time, of course. But it was an amazing lull, he thought, with everyone in the world seemingly someplace else. Where were all the people?

He picked up the binoculars and scanned the far shore. He looked for the sailboat with the red sail he had seen earlier, but it was nowhere to be found. Upper lake, he figured, or perhaps it had slipped into one of the bays whose mouths could not easily be seen from across the lake. He scanned more of the far shore and located the tri-hull. It abruptly banked away from shore toward center lake, and from the rise and fall of the bow Art saw that it had been given full-throttle. He could remember the powerful sensation and rush of excitement from when he had driven one.

The tri-hull was on an intercept course with the wharf, though it would take a few minutes to cover the distance. That tri-hull would cover it quicker than most, Art knew. He glanced again with the binoculars: the driver was hard to see. On it came until, as Art expected, the throttle was chopped as it approached the safety buoy line. It was a no wake zone inside the buoys and that tri-hull produced a big wake. Drivers who violated the zone were tracked down by Billy Teague and issued tickets. No one looked the other way on that one. It was dangerous on busy days with many boats circling in holding patterns as though airliners at O'Hare.

The tri-hull was idling now and angling to pull alongside the wharf. The driver sat low, but Art could see he wore a dark baseball cap and a dark shirt. Art eased out of his chair and leaned against the gas pump at the end of the wharf, ready to receive the boat as it moored.

As the boat pulled alongside, Art was stunned to see that the driver wore a uniform exactly like his old uniform as the Chief. Art pulled his hand back from reaching for the boat and stood up. The man took off his cap and looked up at Art with a smile and Art saw himself. The driver was Art, in his Chief uniform.

Art took a step back and looked away a moment, but when he looked back he still saw himself sitting behind the wheel in the boat.

Something stirred in the back of the boat and abruptly someone sat up and then stood up. It was Nathan Bedford and he had a wide, maniacal grin. He reached down to the seat and brought up a double-barreled shotgun and pointed it at Art.

"How's your summer going, Chief?" Bedford said.

And then he fired.

Art nearly fell off the sofa when he woke up. He caught himself and then sat up quickly and looked around. It took a moment for him to focus. His palms were sweaty and so was his forehead. The dream had been vivid. He usually forgot dreams quickly, but this one lingered. He could still hear the shotgun blast and see Bedford's face. He glanced at his watch: Carolyn would be home soon. He had slept longer than he realized. He sat on the edge of the sofa, looking around the room and soaking up its familiarity. He wiped his sweaty palms on his shorts.

After a while, he went to the kitchen and drank some water and leaned against the sink a few minutes. Then he made himself a Laphroaig on the rocks and went out to the dock. He grasped the dock railing and looked across the lake to the marina. Everything was normal. The world was as it should be. He sipped the peaty scotch, and it woke him up. He scanned the lake again. There was no tri-hull Evinrude lurking. A fleet of sailboats with yellow and orange sails swarmed toward the dam end of the lake. One of his neighbors further down their bay waved as he cruised by in his boat and headed out the bay's mouth. Art managed a smile and wave, tried to appear casual, relaxed. He raised his scotch glass to try to be more convincing. The man saluted him in return.

Coming out of the house, he'd still had a bit of a chill from the dream and so he sat at the edge of his dock and let the sun warm his shoulders and legs as he sipped scotch and dangled his feet over the side just above the water. He watched his neighbor's boat speed away from the bay out into the lake. The scotch and sun warmed him up. He felt much better. It had been a nasty, unexpected dream. But just a dream. No need to read too much into a dream. Dreams were dreams. Everybody had them. He looked again at his watch. He would tell Carolyn all about it when she got home. And about Bedford, too. He should have told her about that sooner. He had not wanted to worry her, to involve her.

He finished the scotch and sat the glass beside him and leaned back and stared up at the sun, eyes closed. Its warmth and the glow from the scotch had restored him. What a ridiculous dream, he thought. He wondered, though, about the symbolism of seeing himself driving Bedford to the marina. Did that mean he deserved what he got? Did it mean he delivered Bedford to himself because he owed Bedford something? No—he owed

Bedford nothing. It was just a fucking dream. He was no expert on them, but he believed that sometimes dreams were just random thoughts flowing together. Half-baked notions that someone would have proper control of if they were awake. He wondered if Walt Holden would agree but concluded that he didn't really care.

For a while, he watched several boats slowly pull alongside the marina wharf across the lake. It was too far to make out people, but he was sure Pete Armstrong must be one of them standing on the wharf. Next season *he* would be on that wharf. As he watched, he heard a car pull into the drive and then a car door being closed. He thought for a moment about how to explain his dream to Carolyn.

But when he got up and turned around, he saw Red walking toward him across the wide lawn.

Twenty-Seven

Red wasn't smiling as he walked across the yard toward Art. Mostly he looked down at the grass. He walked briskly. Art knew something was up.

"What is it?" Art said.

"Bedford's back." Red plunged his hands into his pockets. "The bastard."

Art didn't say anything. He could still hear the shotgun blast from the dream.

"Did you hear me, Art?"

"I hear you fine. Bedford's back. I know."

"You do? Did you see him?"

"Sort of."

"Where? Scotty saw him eating at Bunnie's a while ago. Has he been out here?"

Art decided against telling Red about the dream. It would just be an unnecessary distraction. And hard to explain.

"Is someone keeping track of him?" Art said.

"Scotty is. I'm going to haul him in. I just wanted to talk to you first."

"If you're going to just haul him in, why talk to me?"

Red pulled his hands from his pockets and placed them on his hips.

"Technically, you're still Chief, Art. That's why."

Art nodded.

"But it sounds like you have your mind made up."

"I still work for you, Art. It's still your call."

Art wished, of course, that it wasn't his call at all. He wished it would just go away. He was tired of making the calls. He would have preferred to get a second scotch and sit back down on the dock. But that now seemed unlikely.

"My call, right," Art said.

He turned and looked back across at the marina for a moment. He thought of just dumping it back into Red's lap. After all, he would be Chief in mere weeks. It was very tempting. Red would handle it. He just had to give the word, the order. No one would question it. But he couldn't. He just wasn't built that way. He sighed heavily.

"Okay, Red. Let me go put some pants on. No Chief was ever really Chief wearing shorts and flip-flops."

Art followed Red into Argus. At the station, he called Bill and Red into his office. It *was* still his office. For a few more weeks, anyway. Red had been prudent about not using it and still worked from his own desk out with Bill and Scotty.

"What have we heard from Scotty?" Art said.

"He called in a few minutes ago," Bill said. "He followed Bedford out of town, from Bunnie's. And Bedford isn't driving a rental. This time he has an old blue Ford pickup, an F100. Indiana plates."

"Plenty of old trucks around here," Art said. "Blends in easier, except for the plates."

"Have you run the plates yet, Bill?" Red said.

Yes, Art thought. *Good call. Part of the process.*

"I was getting ready to," Bill said.

"Go on and do that now if you will," Red said. "Thanks, Bill.

Bill glanced quickly at Art but then got up and left.

Art was impressed. Red sounded like a Chief—acted like a Chief.

"Maybe it's stolen," Red said "You never know. That would be an easy out."

"Could be," Art said. "Likely not, but only lazy cops wouldn't check."

Art thought, *I still hold the title, but Red has the edge now. I still have experience, though.*

"We cover all the bases," Red said. "We study all the angles."

"And who taught you that?"

"You did, Art." Red grinned.

"You're ready for this job," Art said. "You do realize that, don't you?"

"Yeah, I do. But how about you? Are you ready for what comes next?"

"You mean Bedford?"

"No. I meant your new life. Not being Chief anymore."

"I'm eager," Art said. "And ready, too. There's just this last thing."

"Bedford," Red said. "He stands in your way."

"I guess he does. I guess he has something on his mind. He didn't come back for the fishing. So, he stands in my way and we stand in his. Something will have to give. It can't be us."

"I know that. And you're not just going to let me handle it, are you, Art?"

Art shook his head slowly.

"No. I can't."

"Why not?"

"Because a man is measured by his very last days at something far more than all the days that came first."

"People won't care, Art. Not really. They'd remember your long years of service."

"No, mostly they wouldn't. A very few might, sure. But plenty wouldn't. Besides, it's not about what they might think, ultimately. It's about what I'd think of myself. This last thing falls on me. I'm still Chief."

"Okay. I hear you. What do you want me to do?"

"Be my top deputy just a little longer."

"I can do that. Tell me what you need me to do."

"I need you to be patient."

"I can do that, too."

"Can you also stay out of my way when I ask?"

Red looked away, at the window.

"Okay, Art."

"And don't second-guess me."

Red nodded.

Bill came back into Art's office.

"The truck's his."

Red shrugged.

"It was worth checking," Art said. "Sometimes you snag someone that way. Part of the process."

"Now what?" Bill said.

Red started to speak but stopped himself and looked at Art.

"Get Scotty on the horn, Bill," Art said. "Find out where Mr. Bedford is right damn now."

"On it, boss," Bill said as he left the room.

Art opened a desk drawer, retrieved his revolver, loaded it, and placed it in the holster and then on his hip.

One last time, he was the Chief again.

Twenty-Eight

As Art pulled into Bunnie's, he was thoroughly blindsided by déjà vu: Scotty was picking himself up off the parking lot. Jesus H. *Christ,* Art thought as he got out, remembering fifteen years before when Dominick Cruikshank lay bleeding in almost the same spot. Lightning had somehow struck twice. How was it possible?

Scotty was bent over, clutching his pants with his hands, breathing hard. He looked up at Art. His face was red and his shirt was pulled out of his pants on one side.

"He's got my gun," Scotty said hoarsely. "He jumped me and popped me one good."

"How long, Scotty?" Art was already edging away and scanning the lot and the houses beyond it. He had his hand on his revolver.

"Maybe a minute or so. No more. He slipped around the back."

"Call Red and wait for him," Art said as he walked toward the corner of the tavern. Behind it were the same woods where he had had to kill Brant Russell. Like father, like son? He sure hoped not. He glanced back once at Scotty, who looked utterly lost and was slowly trying to tuck his shirt back in. Thank God Bedford hadn't shot Scotty in the struggle.

"I'm sorry, Art," Scotty called, but Art didn't turn around a second time. There would be plenty of time to analyze it all later. He hoped. Scotty had screwed up somehow, but that didn't matter much now. What was done was done and now events had been set into motion. So be it. He was tired of dancing with Bedford.

As he eased toward the corner of the building and slowly peered around it, Art felt a strange sense of calm. *This thing is going to get cleaned up, and I'm going to do the cleaning*, he thought. Art understood that he would have to be Chief on his last day just as much as on the first. And this was the last day, he knew. If he survived this little dance with Bedford, he was done. No more riding out the last weeks just for appearances and transitions and such. He would hand his gun to Red and walk away.

If he survived. He knew that he might not. He had dodged fate and bullets for a long time, and maybe it would finally be his time. Maybe God, or whoever it was that actually ran things, had it in mind that this was Art's last day on Earth. *Maybe so,* Art thought. *And maybe not.* But there was no turning away from it. Twenty-five years of good service was riding on it. You're only as good as your last day at something, he reminded himself again. Steve Parnell had drilled that into him in Chicago.

Art slipped around the corner to the nearest tree trunk and slowly peered around it. He surveyed the woods ahead. They were thick and still green, even though fall was creeping closer. He forced himself with some effort to not think of Brant Russell. Focus on what's here and now—what's ahead. And watch the flanks, damnit. Don't get flanked. Russell was dead. Long dead. Fifteen years of dead. Really, really dead. This was the son, up ahead somewhere, and he's a different animal, likely. Was he? No way to know.

He slowly pulled out his revolver. There was no putting that off. He should have done it before he even left the lot. That was rust, maybe. Indecision? He hoped not. Indecision was deadly. Indecision got plenty of folks killed as dead as Russell. Big time dead. He looked around the tree again: nothing. A slight breeze made the treetops swish back and forth. He hoped Scotty would obey him and stay put and wait for Red.

He knew that Scotty must have pushed, must have confronted Bedford—provoked him. That would come from loyalty. Scotty would have been just trying to look out for his Chief. He knew Scotty was a good man, a good father to a little girl, but he had never really seen serious trouble. He had probably been ripe for the picking. Whatever it was that drove Bedford, it had been enough to give him an edge over a small-town deputy whose only real fight might have been over a girl in high school. *But I'm not Scotty,* Art reminded himself. *This ain't my first rodeo. We'll see.*

Art stepped from behind the tree and into the woods. He stopped every few steps and listened for sounds, but it was very quiet. Too quiet. He kept going until he reached the creek and beyond it the spot where Russell had died. Don't think about that, he told himself. Make that ancient history and focus. Look for signs. He did look around and saw a place where plants had been trampled: Bedford had come this way. Art kneeled behind a tree trunk and checked his front and then his flanks. Remember those damn flanks. That's where Lee should have been looking at Gettysburg, at his flanks, instead of obsessing over that damn center. That center undid him on the third day. *I'm not Lee*, Art thought. *I'll do it the easy way if I can and avoid a costly frontal assault. I won't go like Pickett did and get slaughtered for no reason except to say he made the glorious charge and carried out Lee's orders.* Art looked up: he heard birds chirping again and felt it signaled that Bedford was further on, deeper into the woods, which stretched several miles away from town.

He watched and waited. The birds kept singing. Good. Excellent. He could hear squirrels scampering along branches above him. He choked back memories of Russell. He didn't like the idea of being sucked deeper into the woods. It suddenly seemed very wrong, like Lee ordering Pickett to sacrifice his division out of stubbornness. Art wasn't stubborn or reckless and cared nothing for the sort of glory Pickett so desperately wanted on his day of reckoning with history. Art wanted to re-assess the situation. It just didn't feel right. Was that fear? Sure. But also prudent.

After a while the decision was final: he worked his way back toward Bunnie's, walking backwards from tree to tree, careful to keep his revolver in a firing position. He watched those damn flanks like a hawk.

As he slipped back out of the woods, he saw Red looking around the corner of the tavern, his gun raised. Art waved and Red lowered his gun. Art holstered his and moved to a tree next to the tavern corner so he could talk to Red.

"Did you see him?" Red said.

"No. How's Scotty?"

"Embarrassed. Sorry."

"But alive," Art said.

"That, too. I posted him at the other side of the building, in case Bedford doubles back that way."

"That's good thinking, Red. Does Scotty have a weapon, though?"

"The shotgun from my car."

More good thinking, Art thought. Red was going to be okay as Chief. There would be growing pains, but Art felt that he had what it takes. But Art didn't want Red to have to start his tenure by shooting someone. If that had to happen, it was on Art. Another responsibility that fell on him and could not be delegated. With luck, Red might never have to shoot anyone.

"What's the plan?" Red said.

"I'm working on that."

"I'm right here, Art."

"I know it. Thanks."

What *was* the plan? To stop Bedford, of course, without anyone getting shot. Including Bedford, if possible. There were possibilities: Bedford might simply give up after a brief romp in the woods. Perhaps unlikely, but possible. Bedford might shoot himself and solve the problem for them. Unlikely, though it wasn't unheard of for a cornered and unbalanced person to take their own life under pressure. Was Bedford unbalanced? Misguided, perhaps. No way to know. The other possibility, of course, was that Art would have to either capture or kill Bedford. Likely. That was the plan.

"First things first," Art said. "Red, go in Bunnie's. Sarge keeps a thirty-eight under the counter. Take it to Scotty and bring the shotgun to me. On the way back, grab some extra thirty-eight rounds and shotgun shells from your car."

"Okay. You want Scotty to stay where he is?"

"I do. If Bedford tries to double back for a car, he has to come back through here. He may try that."

"What about Bill?"

Art thought a moment.

"Yeah, call Bill and get him out here, too. And call the county sheriff. Might as well let him know we're earning our pay today. We're already pushing his jurisdiction."

Red left, and Art checked the cylinder of the revolver. He knew it was loaded, but he wanted to see the bullets. He wanted to know they were there, ready. The plan wasn't so much of a plan. Bedford had a gun and six bullets. Art planned to have more bullets than he did and a shotgun, too.

And better luck.

As he waited, he thought of Carolyn. He wondered what she was doing at that moment. He glanced at his watch. Maybe getting ready to go home. He hoped he would be seeing her again. He couldn't imagine that he wouldn't, but one never knew in shitty deals like this. It was hard to do, but he forced himself to mostly block her out. He couldn't afford to be distracted or have feelings. Those things could get someone killed in a deal like the one about to unfold.

For a while, he moved over to the corner of the building and kept an eye on the woods. Better cover and only one flank to deal with. Then Red came back and handed Art the shotgun, extra shells, and more thirty-eight rounds. Art tried to make light of it.

"Maybe I need one of those bandoliers, Red, like some desperado riding with Pancho Villa. And maybe a sombrero."

Red smiled.

"You're loaded for bear, Art. For sure."

Art studied Red's face.

"You do know who Pancho Villa was, right?"

"I'll make a note to read up on him when we have some more free time."

Art grinned and offered a hand. They shook, and then Art checked the safety on the shotgun. He clicked it off.

"So, you're just going to go in and find him," Red said. "That's pretty much the plan?"

"Pretty much. If I could call in an air strike, I would. Though the city council might not be too happy about that. A couple of those folks own land out here."

"That's funny, Art. They say a sense of humor is a man's best weapon."

"I believe it. But I'll still keep the shotgun."

"You sure about all this, Art?"

"No, but there's no alternative, really. It's our problem to fix. I'm still Chief. That makes it mostly *my* problem to fix."

"I could go with you," Red said. "More firepower."

"Or more targets for Bedford. Depends on how you look at it. But you stay here, Red. Scotty's too shook up. If Bedford slips back, it falls on you."

"I don't like it."

"Hell, neither do I. I'd rather be sipping scotch on my boat dock. But it's the hand that got dealt. Time to play it out."

"Maybe he'll just surrender," Red said hopefully.

"Maybe he will. Funny things happen every damn day."

Art winked at Red and then slipped back into the woods.

The shotgun made Art feel a little better about his chances. In a fire fight he could overwhelm Bedford with it, maybe make him fire his six rounds quickly—and poorly. When he reached the creek, he was being more observant, more focused than the first trip in, and he thought he saw where Bedford had crossed, and then he picked up a few footprints on the other side.

As he walked from tree to tree, cautiously looking ahead and watching for movement on his flanks, too—*don't forget your damn flanks*—he wondered what had gotten into this boy. If he really never knew his dad, what was the big deal? Where did this allegiance come from? It was one thing to be curious about a dead father and to go see where he died. Art understood that well enough. That would be a natural feeling and Art wouldn't begrudge that of anyone. But following a Chief around, that crossed the line. And now he had assaulted one of his deputies and taken a gun. Now it was criminal. Serious. And this boy may have worked himself into a corner with no way out.

Was there a way out? Well, the boy could surrender. Just call out that he was done running and toss out the gun and everybody goes home, except Bedford, who is headed for jail or a grave. His choice. *Would* he surrender? Well, Art would try to get him to if he could make contact without any shots fired. Once the first bullet flies, though, the equation changes. Then Art would be required to return fire. Deadly force.

Art figured he was about a quarter mile into the woods. Plenty of woods left. They stretched another couple miles. There was a road and some clear land on the other side, no cover, and he knew the county sheriff would set up shop over there once Red had filled him in some more. That was county jurisdiction over there. If the county boys took Bedford, fine. But Art was going to push it all the way to the end of the woods if that's what it took.

But it might not go that far. Things could come to a head at any time well before the woods ran out. What had happened back in Bunnie's lot, Art suspected, was likely not planned. Scotty's zeal to do his job had surely sparked a confrontation, and then things slipped out of control. Bedford might even have legitimately feared for his life. But once things got going, they often kept going. Bedford may not have meant to assault Scotty and take the gun, but he had. Perhaps consumed by fear and anxiety, the boy had run off with the gun—into the same damn woods where his father had died. *Too damn weird*, Art thought. Maybe the boy would calm down enough soon and see things differently. Maybe there was enough reason in him to eventually toss the gun. Maybe, maybe, maybe. But nothing was certain.

Art wondered what Bedford was thinking. Was he thinking about his father? How strange it would be if Bedford was imagining his father being pursued by Art. Was Bedford obsessed with re-enacting the killing of his father? Art couldn't understand that. Was Bedford crazy? No way to know at this point. And it didn't matter all that much. All that mattered was for Art to bring him out, alive if possible. Alive would be best. Art didn't want the burden of dead.

Could he really do it? Art paused behind a thick tree. Hell of a time to be unsure about pulling the trigger. But doubt had filled him up. He looked ahead and listened. Nothing. What the fuck was he doing out here in these damn woods? Well, he was the Chief. No, that was now just a word. A word with little meaning for Art. It did not accurately define him anymore. What did?

"Jesus," he said. "Hell of a time to become a philosopher." It came out rather loud, and he worried that if Bedford was close, he could have heard him. He looked back. He was pretty sure no one back there could have heard him. The woods would contain his words. Seal them in. They had sealed him in.

He moved ahead, to another thick tree. So, he wasn't retreating after all. He was glad to know that. If he went back empty-handed, he would be defeated. All the days before this one no longer existed. Only this day mattered.

Art was surprised by where his thoughts had drifted: to the Frost poem. What a time to think about a poem. And then he looked around, at all the tall, thick trees:

Whose woods these are I think I know
And:
The woods are lovely, dark and deep
But I have promises to keep,
And miles to go before I sleep,
And miles to go before I sleep.

It was a hell of a poem. No matter how often he read it, it amazed him. So simple and yet also so dense, complicated. Cold and dark, too. Carolyn had told him the poem wasn't really about suicide so much, and that the narrator resists any notion of death and such. But in places, it sure sounded deadly enough to Art.

And now here he was in woods just as lovely, dark and deep. And with his own promises to keep. And even several miles to go before he could sleep.

But he wasn't thinking about sleeping.

Art wished he had brought some water. He could go back to the creek, but that was more than a quarter-mile. Perhaps now closer to half a mile. And doing so could make him the pursued instead of the pursuer. So, that was out. And how would he explain it if something happened while he went looking for water? It would be unexplainable. Unthinkable. Thank goodness it was not a hot day. He could go without water. He had no choice.

He looked at his watch: he'd been in the woods more than an hour. He kept moving forward, slowly, stopping regularly to listen for any sound, but all he heard were the birds, the squirrels. Even the earlier breeze had gone somewhere else, and the tops of the trees were still. He judged himself to be a full mile into the woods. There was a ravine ahead, and Art moved toward it cautiously. Ambush country.

Should he just call out for Bedford? Maybe call for his surrender? No, that sounded like something out of a movie. A bad movie. Hollywood loved making the chase a black-and-white issue: brave men hunting an evil cretin and all that. But the truth was that it was about scared men stumbling around in woods, and no one really sure about what would happen. It was like combat on a smaller, more contained scale. He thought of Dominick. Dom would know what this was about. He had seen some action in those jungles over in Vietnam. Dom might tell him to go home, let the county sheriff handle it, and live a long life with your wife. That was the lesson Dom had learned about combat: it wasn't worth getting killed over.

Art wiped sweat off his forehead and then wiped his hands on his pants. He gripped the shotgun tightly and moved toward the ravine. He didn't relish having to cross the ravine. He would be exposed and quite vulnerable, especially climbing up the far slope. It would be a little like Pickett and his Virginians crossing that long and open field to their deaths. But he had no choice. There was a solid tree at the ravine's edge and he crawled over to it.

Art looked down along the ravine to the right but didn't see anything. To the left, though, perhaps one hundred yards away, he saw something—a flash of colors: white and blue. Whatever it was, it was partially hidden by tall weeds. He wasn't sure what he was seeing but knew he would have to go for a closer look to rule it out. He didn't dare move deeper into the woods and beyond the ravine with anything on his flanks that might be Bedford. It was probably nothing, some debris left by hikers, perhaps, or from kids who had been smoking weed and drinking beer, but he had to make sure.

Instead of slipping down the slope into the ravine, he chose the more prudent option: working his way along the tree line on the lip of the slope. Much better cover. He would command high ground from the top of the slope. In the ravine he would be a sitting duck. He thought once again of Lee and Gettysburg: *you should have taken that high ground the first day, general, while you still could. It proved your undoing.* Art would not make that mistake.

He moved along the ravine's lip slowly, pausing behind trees and taking looks at what was ahead. He kept the shotgun pointed in front of him. It could blunt any sudden attack, he felt. To win a fight, have more firepower than the other guy. It wasn't complicated. And don't make mistakes. Don't walk into anything. Check it out.

Halfway along, he still could not decide what the object was. He halted for a moment and kneeled, the shotgun still at the ready, and looked around and listened. Nothing moved. There were no sounds. The woods were lovely, dark, and quiet, he thought. Well, not so dark. A good amount of light seeped in. He thought of the county sheriff, likely well ahead at the end of the woods, perhaps waiting with some of his boys to see what Art might drive to them. It was sort of like pheasant hunting, in a way.

He thought of his own men, well behind him. By now Bill was there with Scotty and Red. He hoped Red would not get impatient and try to join him. A few months ago that might have been the case, he figured, but now, Red seemed far more seasoned, measured—thoughtful. He guessed Red would hold his position and keep Bill and Scotty in line, too. That would be the mark of a Chief.

He moved on, slowly, glancing often at the blue and white object ahead. He was getting closer to it, but still could not decide what it was. Then, when he closed in on it and was directly opposite it from the ravine's lip, looking down, he saw that it was a body. A man. He kept the shotgun aimed at the body and watched to see if it would move. He had been very quiet and perhaps had not been heard. He could not see the head clearly and wondered if the man was sleeping. He did not know what Bedford was wearing. This man wore blue jeans and a white t-shirt. If it was Bedford, how odd for him to take a nap.

Art watched the body for a minute, the shotgun pointed at it. Nothing. He was tempted to fire once in the air. That would be a very dramatic entrance. A hell of a wake-up call. But the shot might be heard by others and cause Red, or the county sheriff, to enter the woods, creating more targets, more chances for confusion and accidents. There were consequences and reactions to every motion.

How could Bedford sleep at a time like this? And who else could it be? Art had read that American soldiers fighting in Normandy in World War II sometimes fell asleep in combat from sheer exhaustion and stress. Some fell asleep sitting up.

Art edged all the way down the slope into the ravine and crouched at the bottom, the shotgun up to his shoulder now and ready to fire. The man still did not move, and Art slowly moved toward him and tapped his shoes with the barrel of the shotgun. Nothing. The body was on a slight bump in the ground, the head lower than the rest of it and surrounded by weeds. Then it occurred to him that the position of the legs didn't seem right. One leg was tucked under the other at an angle that would not be comfortable for long. He lunged forward, the shotgun pointed at the head and saw that it was indeed Bedford. A very dead Bedford, with a neat little hole at the temple and eyes staring forever toward the sky. He stepped over the body and saw the other temple, much of it blown out by the bullet. That was where most of the blood was.

He stood over the body a minute, trying to make sense of what had happened. That eluded him and he walked over to a fallen tree trunk and sat down with the shotgun across his lap, and after a couple more minutes, he cried.

Art wasn't sure how long he had sat on the log. Perhaps ten minutes, maybe less. He got up slowly and took another look at Bedford's face. The boy's mouth seemed twisted a little—almost like someone sleeping with their mouth open. It reminded him of the dead in Civil War photographs, except Bedford was there in living color—dead color, that is. That made no sense, dead color. Could there be such a thing as dead color? Art tried to be objective for a moment—tried to be the Chief—and wondered whether somehow it could have been merely an accident.

But he didn't think many people ever accidentally shot themselves in a temple. Maybe Bedford had, somehow. Nothing surprised him about people anymore. The coroner might put two and two together from the wound and how close the gun was and make it clear that suicide was the only answer. That seemed most likely to Art. He had seen only one other suicide, a young woman in Chicago when he was a beat cop: she had slit her wrists in a bathtub. The bath water was red and had colored her pubic hair red, too. He never knew why she had done it. She didn't leave a note.

And now he had Bedford and no answer as to what compelled him to do it. Maybe he panicked, felt overwhelmed. Maybe he was depressed for a long time. All this for a dead father he had never met? Art couldn't fathom it. And he knew there was no use trying. It was what it was and no more. But he felt sorrow. Lots of it. He hated to think that even in a small way he was responsible for the boy's death, but he knew that in that small way, he indeed was.

He looked around at the trees, the only witnesses to Bedford's last minutes. He thought of the Frost poem and what Carolyn had said about it not really being about death. But here in these woods, everything was about death.

Art started to lean over and retrieve Scotty's revolver, lying next to the body; then he remembered that it was part of a crime scene. He didn't like the idea of leaving a loaded gun on the ground, but it had to stay for now. He looked at Bedford's face a last time, for a lingering moment, but he knew it was a face he likely would never forget. It would go into the gallery in his mind, along with Brant Russell and Margo Townsend. They could all keep each other company.

He ejected all the shells from the shotgun and picked them up and put them in his pants pocket. He didn't want to carry a loaded shotgun anymore. Not ever again. He remembered his revolver and took it from the holster and unloaded it, too, and put the bullets in his shirt pocket. He thought about whacking the shotgun against the nearest tree trunk. But that was silly, really. Emotional. And it was department property. It would make paperwork for Red. And it would be something to explain that would be hard to explain. An act that would leave many people unsatisfied. It would be how Art was remembered, and so he clutched the shotgun with one hand and started back out of the woods the way he had come.

As he walked, he wondered what might have happened had Bedford put up a fight. Could he have killed the boy? He had told Dr. Holden that he couldn't kill anyone ever again. Was that true? He hoped never to have it put to the test again. He couldn't imagine that he would ever have to. Art was sorry that the boy had felt he had to take his own life, but he was thankful that it had not been his duty to take it. There was a small acorn of comfort in that. A fine line. It wasn't much, but Art felt it was something to build on.

Twenty-Nine

When Art emerged from the woods, a light rain fell. It was soothing, gentle—almost caressing. Maybe it would wash away his sins, he joked to himself. Maybe not. Did he have many sins? Not so many. And time would deal with what he had. His sins did not run deep. But the rain felt cool and good, and he felt an odd sense of relief. He handed the shotgun to Red, who was still holding his own revolver.

"You can holster that pistol, Red. Bedford's dead."

Art sighed long and heavily.

Red looked confused. He glanced at the thick woods.

"I didn't hear anything."

"Neither did I. But he's dead all right. Dead as dead can be. I came across his body halfway in—one shot to the temple. End of story."

"He shot himself? Why?"

Art shrugged.

"Maybe he just couldn't take it anymore, whatever it was that bothered him so much. I don't know. We'll never know, I guess. He just did. People just do."

"I'll be damned," Red said.

"I hope not," Art said. "Anyway, call our good friend the sheriff. I figure Bedford's body is in the county. They can bring him out. I don't want any part of that."

Red finally managed to holster his revolver.

"I don't understand why we didn't hear the shot," Red said. "You say you didn't hear it, either?"

Art shook his head.

"Woods can hide lots of noise," Art said. "George Pickett didn't hear his whole division fighting at Five Forks, just a short distance away. An acoustic anomaly is what it's called, I believe."

"Pickett," Red said. "Sounds like some more reading to do."

Art smiled, placed a hand on Red's shoulder.

"You're learning—Chief."

Art took off his holster and revolver and handed them to Red. He fished in his pockets for the shotgun shells and bullets and handed them over, too.

"Department property, Red. My uniforms—I'll keep them as souvenirs."

"Like old Army uniforms," Red said.

"Yeah—just like. Something to gather dust in a closet."

"Now what? Do you just ride off into the sunset?"

"That sounds pretty good to me. I believe I will."

Art shook hands with Red and smiled.

"You know where to find me when you want to go fishing, Chief Foley."

"That I do," Red said. "That I do."

Art walked away but looked back once, smiled again, and tossed Red a sloppy salute. Red returned it crisply.

In the parking lot, Art briefly explained to Scotty and Bill what had happened in the woods and then he shook hands with them.

"Don't take any wooden nickels, boys."

"Okay, Art," Bill said. "You take care, Chief."

"I'll take it any way I can get it," Art said. "And the Chief is standing over there."

Art pointed to Red, who waved.

Scotty stared at the ground.

"Chin up, Scotty," Art said. "Learn from all this. You're a good man."

Art patted his shoulder.

"Thanks." Scotty said. "I appreciate it."

"The truth is easy to say. We'll drink a beer to it one of these days, Scotty."

"Okay, Art. We sure will."

Art opened the door of his car and looked back at Bill and Scotty. He let his gaze linger on them a moment and enjoyed seeing them. In a way, they were like sons to him. Red, too. Especially Red.

"Gents, come out to the house when you get a chance, and you can pick up the car," he said. "But not today."

Thirty

Art got home before Carolyn. She was a little late, but he wasn't concerned. She often had things come up at the end of a school day. He didn't quite know what to do with himself when he first walked into the house. He looked in the refrigerator, but concluded he wasn't really hungry yet. He knew he would be very hungry later, after he decompressed, as Steve Parnell would call it. He thought of calling Stevie to tell him it was finally over, that now he, too, was no longer a cop, that he had finally reached the last stop. But he decided there was plenty of time for that. No hurry. None in the world.

He remembered that he was sweaty and dirty and needed a shower, and so he soaked in the shower a long time and then slipped into crisp, clean shorts and a fresh t-shirt and stepped into his flip-flops. He looked out the kitchen window and saw the rain had let up. It had never really gotten started properly and had been at best a fine mist. Now the sun was trying to peek from under a large gray cloud.

After the shower, he felt he had washed away more than dirt and sweat. Not his sins, he cautioned himself, but surely much of his burden. What was his burden? Being Chief. Having to appear strong. The requirement of being wise, in control. An image no one could really live up to without paying a price.

Art had paid that price for decades. But he had survived it all, too, and that was his reward, he figured. Do we live our lives for rewards? He thought it might be better if we lived our lives because they were worth living and could be joyous. But rewards were okay, too. *Keep them in perspective*, he reminded himself.

But make them small.

Like a veteran of a war—one who had truly been in the thick of things—Art knew he would always be proud of his time as Chief. It was a way he could never be again, but he had been it and done it as best as was possible when it had needed to be done. That sounded funny to him, but he felt in his heart it was right. The wording didn't have to be elegant.

Art made himself a Laphroaig on the rocks and walked out to the boat dock and sat on the edge of it. The sun had finally eluded the cloud and the day brightened and the water sparkled. He looked across the lake at the marina. A boat was pulling alongside the wharf. But Art didn't want to think much about the marina. Not yet. Let all that come later, when it was time.

He sipped the scotch and felt the warmth as it flowed into him. He touched the cold, wet glass to his forehead and rubbed it across slowly. It had been some day. One for the books. One for the ages.

He thought of poor Bedford, lying in a bloody heap of his own doing. How sad. It was tragic. And how strange. Who was Bedford? Art would never know because he certainly had no plans to find out any more than what he knew, which was that the man was dead. That was all he needed to know. Poking around in it would not be profitable. He couldn't change anything. Time to move on ahead to find out what waited for him in the future.

But yes, he felt sorrow for Bedford. Sorrow and sorry. He knew it was more complicated than that, that he would think of the boy from time to time. But each time, he suspected—and hoped—he would think of him with a heart less heavy. There really was no other way to look at it. Maybe there was, but Art didn't care to explore alternatives. Sometimes it was best to just go with what you knew and bank on time and hope to help soften the rough edges.

He heard a car pull in the driveway and then heels tapping on the driveway, the back door opening and shutting, and knew it was Carolyn. He smiled. Those were great sounds. The best sounds. She would eventually come looking for him, as she always did, to ask about his day, but he abruptly finished his scotch and then walked to the house and found her putting groceries in the refrigerator. He watched her for a moment, enjoying the grace in all her movements.

"I heard you coming a ways off," she said without turning around. "Those flip-flops are like snapping fingers."

What a precise image, he thought.

She turned around, smiled, and brushed her blonde bangs away from her face. He smiled, too, and sat his empty scotch glass on the counter.

"You're running late today," he said.

She folded the paper grocery bag and put it into a drawer.

"Tell me about it. I ran into Doris after my last class and she needed to talk—she's pregnant, Art. Can you believe it? She's almost fifty."

"How'd that go?"

"Well, I can tell you she's beside herself. But happy. It's quite a thing to have a baby at her age."

"I guess it would be."

Art tried to picture Carolyn pregnant. That image was fuzzy. He sagged against the counter.

"So, how was your day?" she said. "I heard something about a ruckus over by Bunnie's Tavern, but no details. Anything serious?"

She glanced at a grocery list on the refrigerator door and crossed off some items with a pen.

He hesitated and watched her a moment.

"Nothing Chief Foley can't handle," Art said, glancing quickly at the floor a moment, his arms crossed across his chest. The day flashed across his mind in a jumble. The series of events sailed across his mind quickly like a movie being fast-forwarded.

"Oh?" she said.

"I can fill you in on it all later, Carolyn."

"Was it serious?"

"Serious enough, yes. But later. Not now."

She looked at his face a moment. He felt the scrutiny.

"Calling Red Chief Foley already, are you?"

"Well, it's time. He has the reins now. I walked away—today. I'm done. No going back."

She arched her eyebrows slightly.

"So, that's it," she said. "Wow. Just like that?"

"That's it," he said. "I'm free. Free as a bird."

"Why today, Art?"

He cocked his head slightly.

"I just knew it was time to go. It felt right."

He thought of a line from a song: *Freedom's just another word for nothing left to lose.*

But it was just a random thought, produced by the pressure of the day. He was sure of it. He did not believe the lyrics applied to him. What had Dr. Holden told him? "Doubt is a natural part of any process." Something like that. Doubt, he suspected, reminded you to double check your process.

She sat in a chair at the kitchen table and sighed and kicked off her heels.

"I sure needed to get off my feet. So, you're sure about it, Art—leaving a couple weeks early?"

He managed a sloppy, self-conscious grin and sat down, too.

"The longer I stayed, the harder it would be to say goodbye. It's time to be out of Red's way. As long as I was there, he'd look over his shoulder at me. He doesn't need that. He doesn't need me anymore."

"Is he really up to it?"

Art nodded vigorously.

"Yeah, I believe he is. His Achilles heel will always be impulsiveness. But he's gotten better with it. I struggled with that at first, too. Nobody's perfect. No one *has* to be perfect. That's a trap. A little impulsiveness might even be a good thing—even for a Chief. It makes people human—reminds them they're human. People need to remember that."

"I remember how you were when we first met," she said, grinning. "But impulsiveness is a good thing for a marriage, Art. It keeps a marriage fresh."

She reached across the table and touched his hand. Her touch still thrilled him. It always did. He suspected it always would.

This was his greatest achievement, his marriage to Carolyn. It dwarfed being Chief. It would dwarf owning the marina.

"We do have that, right, Carolyn? Impulsiveness? Still?"

She smiled and pulled blond hair behind a very pink ear.

"What do *you* think?"

He grinned, awkwardly and foolishly at first, and then felt the last bit of the day seep out of him as though he'd had a good workout and everything ugly and evil had been thoroughly sweated out of every pore of his body. Cleansed. Life was like a sauna, he joked to himself.

"How about a scotch?" he said.

She slowly eased back and settled into her chair and Art thought of a satisfied and purring cat stretching to get comfortable.

"I'd love one. But with lots of ice, and a splash of water."

"I can do that," he said.

Art made the drink and sat it on the table in front of her. From behind, he caressed her neck very lightly with both hands. He felt her muscles relax, and she reached a hand behind and grasped one of his, gently.

Art looked up for a moment. From where he stood, he could look out through the living room window and see Lake Argus. The calm blue water was framed nicely, as though on a postcard.

The End

About Michael Loyd Gray

Michael Loyd Gray's stories have appeared in numerous literary journals, including *Alligator Juniper, The Fiction Week Literary Review, Bone Parade, I-70 Review, Westchester Review*, and *Literary Heist*. He is also the author of six novels. *Well Deserved* won the Sol Books Prose Series Prize (2008) and *King Biscuit*, his first YA novel, was released in 2012. Both are set in Gray's fictional small town of Argus, Illinois, which is also the setting for *The Last Stop*. His novel *The Armageddon Two-Step* (2019), won a Book Excellence Award.

Gray earned a MFA in English from Western Michigan University, where he was a Phi Kappa Phi National Honor Society scholar and a fiction editor for *Third Coast*. He served as a staff writer for newspapers in Arizona and Illinois, and currently lives in Kalamazoo, Michigan, where he collects electric guitars (up to a dozen now) and listens intently to blues and vintage rock. Gray teaches creative writing and literature for several colleges when not grappling with a new guitar lick. He has two lazy cats, Suzie Lucifer and Yoda Lucifer."

Also by Michael Loyd Gray

Well Deserved

The folks of Argus, Illinois, from the small-time dealer to the returning Vietnam vet, the townie grocery clerk and the new sheriff, all know what they want out of life, but the paths to their desires are conflicted and unclear. In a narrative with all the clarity and determination of a prophecy, *Well Deserved* chronicles the struggles of these four people as they come to the stark realization that their paths are not solitary, but entwined, and their very lives hinge on one shared moment.

King Biscuit

In *King Biscuit,* Michael Loyd Gray returns once again to the fictional small town of Argus, Illinois, (the setting of his novels *Well Deserved* and *The Last Stop*), to tell a coming-of-age story set in 1966. With the Vietnam War hovering in the background. Seventeen-year-old Billy Ray Fleener, frustrated by the narrow confines of Argus, seeks adventure and a look at the wider world in a novel that puts him on a collision course with the famous as well as infamous.

To learn more about
Flat Sole Studio
and our other projects,
visit us at *flatsolestudio.com*
or scan the QR code below.

www.ingramcontent.com/pod-product-compliance
Lightning Source LLC
Chambersburg PA
CBHW020657120726
47906CB00001B/305